KU-276-938

### Twin Docs' Perfect Match

When Dr. Rob Langley needs an urgent
kidney transplant, his twin brother, Ollie,
steps in to help—changing their lives forever!
As these twin docs start over, it might be time
for them to meet their perfect match!

*Second Chance with Her Guarded GP*

Starting work in a new practice, GP Ollie Langley
hadn't anticipated falling for gorgeous
nurse practitioner Gemma Baxter! Dare he
take a risk on love?

*Baby Miracle for the ER Doc*

When Dr. Rob Langley meets ER doc
Florence Jacobs, sparks fly! And one special night
leads to life-changing consequences.

*Both titles available now!*

NORFOLK ITEM

30129 080 863 773

Dear Reader,

Rob's one of those larger-than-life characters who simply sweeps everyone away with him—and that's precisely what he does to Florence. Neither of them expects to fall in love, and certainly not with someone who's their complete opposite; and neither of them expects their dreams to come true. But thanks to each other, and after a few twists and turns, those dreams really do come true.

Oh, and there's Rob's diagnosis. I'll admit here that I borrowed that from me. I, too, thought I was simply a "busy" person and a bit of a daydreamer with a low boredom threshold; learning there was a reason for it was quite illuminating! And the thing that grounds me is exactly what grounds Rob: the love of someone who's more down-to-earth. I'm very, very grateful for it.

With love,

*Kate Hardy*

# BABY MIRACLE
# FOR THE ER DOC

———

## KATE HARDY

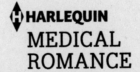

**MEDICAL
ROMANCE**

If you purchased this book without a cover you should be aware that this book is stolen property. It was reported as "unsold and destroyed" to the publisher, and neither the author nor the publisher has received any payment for this "stripped book."

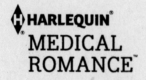

# HARLEQUIN®
## MEDICAL
## ROMANCE™

Recycling programs
for this product may
not exist in your area.

ISBN-13: 978-1-335-40878-5

Baby Miracle for the ER Doc

Copyright © 2021 by Pamela Brooks

All rights reserved. No part of this book may be used or reproduced in any manner whatsoever without written permission except in the case of brief quotations embodied in critical articles and reviews.

This is a work of fiction. Names, characters, places and incidents are either the product of the author's imagination or are used fictitiously. Any resemblance to actual persons, living or dead, businesses, companies, events or locales is entirely coincidental.

This edition published by arrangement with Harlequin Books S.A.

For questions and comments about the quality of this book, please contact us at CustomerService@Harlequin.com.

Harlequin Enterprises ULC
22 Adelaide St. West, 40th Floor
Toronto, Ontario M5H 4E3, Canada
www.Harlequin.com

**Printed in U.S.A.**

**Kate Hardy** has always loved books and could read before she went to school. She discovered Harlequin novels when she was twelve and decided that this was what she wanted to do. When she isn't writing, Kate enjoys reading, cinema, ballroom dancing and the gym. You can contact her via her website, katehardy.com.

## Books by Kate Hardy

### Harlequin Medical Romance

#### *Twin Docs' Perfect Match*
*Second Chance with Her Guarded GP*

#### *Changing Shifts*
*Fling with Her Hot-Shot Consultant*

#### *Miracles at Muswell Hill Hospital*
*Christmas with Her Daredevil Doc*
*Their Pregnancy Gift*

*Unlocking the Italian Doc's Heart*
*Carrying the Single Dad's Baby*
*Heart Surgeon, Prince…Husband!*
*A Nurse and a Pup to Heal Him*
*Mistletoe Proposal on the Children's Ward*
*Forever Family for the Midwife*

Visit the Author Profile page
at Harlequin.com for more titles.

For my readers. Because writing for you
got me through lockdown.

**Praise for
Kate Hardy**

"Ms. Hardy has definitely penned a fascinating
read in this book… Once the hero confesses to the
heroine his plan for a marriage of convenience, I
was absolutely hooked."

—*Harlequin Junkie* on
*Heart Surgeon, Prince…Husband!*

# CHAPTER ONE

ROBERT LANGLEY WALKED through the doors of Asherwick General Hospital.

How good it felt to be back on the side of the hospital where he *belonged*. To be the fixer again, not the fixee.

Not in a helicopter, being evacuated after a burst appendix. Not developing severe blood poisoning that went on to wipe out his kidneys. Not lying in a hospital bed, on dialysis. Not on the operating table, while his twin Oliver was in the operating theatre next door—a living donor, having a kidney cut out for Rob. Not stuck at home after the transplant, with his mother wrapping him in so much cotton wool that he was beginning to resemble a snowman.

The last six months had been tough. Rob had had to come to terms with the fact he'd never again be able to work for the humanitarian aid organisation where he'd volunteered;

with only one working kidney, and a transplanted one at that, he was too much of a potential liability. The mountain rescue team where he volunteered had offered him a support role when he was well enough to come back, but they'd made it clear that he couldn't do the rescue work he'd been used to doing for them. Desk job only.

It had been months since he'd climbed anywhere. Months since he'd done anything riskier than playing chess with his twin. Months since he'd worked—apart from the day the previous weekend when he'd taken Ollie's place among the medics for a sixty-mile fundraising cycle race.

And right now Rob was desperate for a bit of normality. He wanted his life back. His lovely, *busy* life.

He'd taken the first step at the weekend. While he'd been recuperating, he'd let his hair grow out so it was more like his twin's, with his fringe flopping over his eyes, and he'd shaved every day because it was another way of filling the endless seconds until his life went back to normal. But on Saturday morning he'd walked into the barber's and asked them to shave it back to his normal crop, just shy of military barbering. He hadn't shaved for a couple of days. And this morning, when he'd looked in the mirror, he'd seen himself again. Not the patient who could barely do a thing for himself that he'd been forced to be for so long.

His consultant had agreed that Rob wasn't quite ready to go back to climbing, but could go back to work part-time, and now he had a temporary post working three days a week as a registrar in the Emergency Department at Asherwick.

It was so, so good to be back. The fact that nobody knew him here made it all the better, because nobody would fuss that he was overdoing things, or treat him as anyone other than normal.

Rob knew better than to overdo things. The last thing he wanted was to be stuck recuperating again. But it would feel so good to be seen as a doctor first, not as someone recovering from a kidney transplant. To help someone instead of being the one who needed help. To do the job he'd spent years training to do and knew he did well.

'Hello! I wasn't expecting to see you here.'

Rob stared at the woman who'd just spoken to him. He'd never seen this woman in his life before. And he would definitely have remembered her: slight, with dark hair in a pixie cut and huge brown eyes, a heart-shaped face and a generous mouth. She reminded him of a young Audrey Hepburn. All she needed was the little black dress instead of a white coat, the enormous hat and a pair of dark glasses, and she'd be a ringer for Holiday Golightly.

According to her lanyard, she was Dr Florence Jacobs; given they were both in the Emergency Department, it was a fair assumption that she was one of his new colleagues.

Before Rob could apologise for having no idea who she was, she asked, 'How's your patient with chickenpox pneumonia doing?'

'Patient?' What patient? He hadn't treated anyone for months, let alone anyone with chickenpox. Or pneumonia.

She looked disappointed, as if he'd just outed himself as the sort of doctor who couldn't be bothered to remember his patients. Which wasn't who he was at all. 'The elderly woman you brought in, a couple of weeks ago.'

'I'm sorry. I think you must have the wrong person.'

She frowned. 'I'm sure it was you. Just your hair was different.'

His hair was different?

Then the penny dropped.

'Ah. You must mean Oliver. My twin,' he explained. GPs didn't usually bring their patients to the Emergency Department, but Oliver Langley was the kind of doctor who went above and beyond. And Oliver was the sort of person people remembered; he exuded warmth and kindness and made friends in the blink of an eye. 'I can ask him for you, if you like.'

'It's OK. I just…' She flapped a dismissive hand, and a tide of colour swept through her face. 'Never mind.'

Clearly she was embarrassed at making a mistake, and Rob didn't want things to feel awkward between himself and his new colleague. 'Let's rewind that and start again. Good morning. I'm Robert Langley,' he said. 'I'm the new part-time registrar. Rob, to my friends.'

'Florence Jacobs. Senior Reg. Good to meet you.'

Though she didn't offer a shortened version of her a name, he noticed. Did that mean she was the sort who kept a distance between herself and her colleagues? Or did she not like shortening her name?

He shook her hand and his palm tingled.

Uh-oh. That wasn't good.

He was supposed to be concentrating on his new job, not getting side-tracked by attraction. Even if Florence Jacobs was a) single and

b) interested in him, he was only here for a few months before he went back to his old job in Manchester. Although Rob was happy for all his relationships to stay short and sweet, he knew from experience that his girlfriends didn't necessarily see things the same way; there was no guarantee that Florence would be interested in a fling. So it was better to keep things strictly professional rather than act on that pull of attraction he felt towards her. His life had been complicated enough for the last few months. He wanted things kept nice and simple. Just him and his job. No expectations he couldn't fulfil and no girlfriends to be let down when his low boredom threshold kicked in.

'I see they've already given you a lanyard. That's good. Come with me and I'll show you where the staff kitchen is,' she said. 'And you're rostered in Resus with me today, so if there's anything you need just let me know.'

He gave her his best smile. 'Thanks. That'd be great.'

'Welcome to Asherwick General,' she said.

Robert Langley was gorgeous.

Absolutely gorgeous.

Like a young Hugh Grant, without the floppy hair and smooth skin. Though, actually, Flor-

ence rather liked the stubble. And those star-
tling blue eyes, the brighter because there was
no fringe getting in their way. Part of her was
seriously tempted to reach out and touch his
face, find out whether the stubble was spiky
or soft.

But she'd learned the hard way: getting
close to someone netted you a broken heart,
broken dreams and a divorce. So she wasn't
going to act on that flare of attraction to their
new registrar. Besides, looking like that, he
must have women queuing a mile deep to date
him—if he hadn't already been married for
years.

So she switched her head to friendly and
professional mode, smiled and led him through
to the kitchen. 'We have a kitty system here.
Everyone gives their subs to Shobu on Reception once a month and she keeps us stocked
with tea, coffee and stuff. Any special dietary
requirements, just let her know.' She gestured
to the cupboards. 'Mugs and plates are there,
cutlery in the drawer, and if we're lucky it's
someone's birthday and they bring in cake.'

'Or if someone starts in the department
and wants to say hello to his new colleagues,'
Rob said, and placed the carrier bag he'd been
holding on the worktop. 'Cake, cheese straws
and fruit.'

'That,' Florence said with a smile, 'is definitely a good way to say hello.' He'd been thoughtful about it, including things for people who didn't like cake or had other dietary requirements. It was such a nice thing to do, and it made her warm to him.

He took everything out of the bag, including a note.

*Please help yourself!*
*All the best from your new colleague,*
*Rob Langley*

He placed it on the worktop. Then he glanced at his watch. 'We haven't got time for coffee. Not if we want to get a decent handover rather than making people stay on after their shift.'

She liked that, too. He was thinking of their colleagues who were already busy. A team player. Good. That was exactly what they needed. Their last three temps hadn't been team players at all. 'Agreed. Let's go through,' she said.

She introduced him to everyone they passed; and they'd just got to Resus when the red phone shrilled.

Florence answered it, made a few notes, and blew out a breath.

'ETA ten minutes. Elderly patient, fallen and banged his head. He's lost a lot of blood; he collapsed in the ambulance but they've stabilised him,' she said. 'Though he's also a bit confused.'

'So we're looking at an urgent cross-match of blood, getting fluids into him, possibly a transfusion, and then a CT scan from his head to his hip to check for other injuries,' Rob said.

She liked the way his thoughts chimed with hers. 'Exactly.'

Everything was ready by the time their patient arrived.

As the paramedics talked her through what they'd done, she could see that his blood pressure was low, thanks to the blood he'd lost.

'Mr Walker, do you know where you are?' Rob asked.

'I'm not at home, am I?' the elderly man asked, sounding confused.

'No, you're at Asherwick General.'

'My cup of tea…' He looked anxious.

'Do you remember anything that happened?' Florence asked.

'No.' Mr Walker began to shake his head, and stopped, wincing. 'My neck hurts.'

'We think you had a fall and hit your head,' Rob said. 'Your wife's on her way in, with your daughter. I'm Dr Langley, and this is Dr Jacobs. We're going to look after you. I'm just going to take a tiny sample of blood, if that's all right.'

'Yes.' Mr Walker's face crumpled. 'I want Lizzie.'

'She'll be here soon,' Florence reassured him, assuming he meant his wife or his daughter. She glanced at the monitor, deeply unhappy with his blood pressure reading; he'd clearly lost a lot of blood, meaning that not enough was going to his vital organs. 'We're going to get some fluids into you,' she said.

Rob was already on top of it. And he'd done the blood sample without a fuss while they'd been talking to their patient. He might be new and he might only be a temporary colleague, but he was already acting as if he'd been part of the team for years. Unlike their last couple of temps, who'd seemed to wait to be told what to do.

Once Mr Walker was stabilised and they'd stemmed the bleeding, she sent him for an urgent CT scan; then she and Rob went to see his wife and daughter.

'I'm Dr Jacobs and this is Dr Langley,' she introduced them swiftly.

'Lizzie Walker,' his wife said, 'and Jeannette.'

'He was asking for you earlier,' Rob said. 'We told him you were both on your way.'

'Your husband's having a scan at the moment so we can check him over properly and see if he's got any other injuries. He's lost a bit more blood than we'd like, so we're going to give him a transfusion,' Florence said. 'Can you tell us what happened?'

'I'm not sure. He'd gone downstairs to let the dog out and make us both a cup of tea,' Mrs Walker said. 'He must've slipped on the stairs, though I didn't hear him fall. I was in the shower. It was only when I was getting dressed that I heard the dog barking. I thought it was a bit odd, and when I went out I saw Pete lying at the foot of the stairs and there was blood everywhere. I called the ambulance, and I put a blanket over him to keep him warm because I didn't want to risk moving him. He couldn't remember falling, so whether he blacked out or something happened...' She shook her head. 'I don't know. I'm sorry.'

'You did the best thing, keeping him warm and calling the ambulance and not moving him,' Florence reassured her.

'There was so much blood.' Mrs Walker's face was pinched.

'Scalp wounds always seem scary and bleed

a lot,' Rob said, 'because the skin's thicker and there are more veins and arteries. But we've stopped the bleeding now.'

'Is Dad going to be all right?' Jeanette asked.

Florence didn't have enough information to be able to answer that. 'We're looking after him,' she said instead. 'He did seem a little bit confused.' Had he just missed his footing, or had he had a stroke, or was it something else—had he banged his head hard enough to cause an internal bleed? 'Can I ask about his general health before the fall? Any medical conditions?'

'He was fine,' Mrs Walker said.

Jeanette sighed. 'Oh, Mum. That's not quite true. Dad's memory is starting to go a bit.'

'We manage,' Mrs Walker said defensively.

'Nobody's assigning any kind of blame,' Florence said gently. 'We're just trying to put the clues together to work out what happened and what caused it, to help us decide on the best treatment to give him.'

Mrs Walker grimaced. 'We're just getting old. Jeanette's right, Pete's a bit forgetful. He's got high blood pressure, but he takes his medication every day—I bought him one of those weekly pill box things to make sure.' She bit her lip. 'Do you think he had a stroke and that's why he fell? Is that why he can't remember anything?'

'We'll know more when we've seen the scan,' Florence said.

'But if you can give us a full run-down of his medical history, that would really help us work things out,' Rob said, giving her a warm smile.

Mrs Walker and her daughter both seemed to react well to his charm; Florence left him to do the talking and noted down everything they said.

'Thank you—that was very helpful,' she said when they'd finished. 'We'll come and get you as soon as he's back in the department, so you can see him.'

'Stroke?' Rob asked when they'd left the relatives' room.

'Or a bleed on the brain from his fall,' she said. 'I'll be happier when we've seen the scan.'

Mr Walker had just been brought back to the department, and the initial blood tests—pending the full cross-match—meant they were able to start the blood transfusion.

But he was agitated and wouldn't settle.

'Mr Walker, I need you to lie on your back for me and keep your arm still so I can treat you,' Florence said gently. If he kept moving, they wouldn't be able to get the blood into him and the risk of organ failure was growing by the minute.

'My neck hurts,' he said again.

Rob sat next to him and held his hand. 'I know, and we're going to do something about that. But for now we need you to lie still, just for a little while, so we can help you. Florence is going to get you some pain relief, and then we'll bring your wife and your daughter to see you.'

'I can't let them see me covered in blood.' Mr Walker twisted on the bed. 'Not like this.'

'Lie still for us,' she said gently, 'and I'll wash your face so they won't be worried when they see you.'

'Neither of us is going anywhere,' Rob said. 'You're safe. I'm hanging onto you, and Florence will clean you up. So you're perfectly safe to lie still and let us help you. Deal?'

For a moment, Florence thought Mr Walker was going to refuse, but then the fight went out of him. 'All right.'

She and Rob exchanged a glance. Agitation and sudden changes in mood could suggest a stroke or something affecting the patient's ability to process information. Or maybe he was just horribly scared. Until they'd seen the results of that scan, she couldn't be sure.

\* \* \*

Florence gently washed Mr Walker's face, getting rid of all the blood, talking to him all the while. Rob thought how nice she was, how gentle and kind. And he'd noticed that she was calm under pressure; he liked that, too.

He liked his new colleague a lot.

Though he needed to be sensible about it and not act on that attraction. He wasn't great at relationships; plus he was only here for the next three months. As soon as he was fit enough to climb again, he'd be back in his old job in Manchester—the other side of the country. So it'd be better not to start anything in the first place.

Once the scans were back, Florence reviewed them with him. 'I'm glad to see there's no sign of a bleed on the brain or a fracture to the skull,' she said.

They'd done a scan from the top of his head to his hip, to check for other injuries. 'No sign of internal damage or any other fractures either,' Rob said. 'With luck, he'll just have some bruising and that wound on the back of his head.'

'I'm still admitting him so we keep him in overnight for observation,' Florence said. 'I've got a funny feeling. Yes, that confusion could be from the shock of the fall and hitting his head; but, given that his daughter was concerned about memory loss, we need to keep an eye on him.'

'I agree,' Rob said.

Once they'd settled Mr Walker with his family and organised admitting him, they were called to deal with a patient who'd collapsed with a suspected heart attack. He arrested in the middle of Resus, but thankfully they were able to save him and send him up to the cardiac ward.

'I think we're both overdue a break,' Florence said to Rob. 'Would you like to come with me and I'll show you where the canteen is?'

'That'd be nice. Thank you. Coffee is on me,' he added.

'It's your first day, so it's my shout,' she corrected.

'Tell you what—you buy the coffee, I'll buy the cake,' he said.

She smiled. 'That's a deal.'

'Any particular cake you prefer?'

'Cake is cake,' she said.

'Got you.'

In the cafeteria, she bought them both a cappuccino, and he bought two slices of a rich-looking chocolate brownie. 'Ollie—my brother—is a cheese fiend. He doesn't understand what a joy chocolate cake is,' Rob said as they sat down.

'You're right: it *is* a joy—and not just because of the sugar rush,' she said with a smile.

All of a sudden Rob's chest felt too tight. It was nothing to do with his kidney transplant and everything to do with the way that smile transformed her face, changing her from the quiet, capable and serious doctor into someone who was lit up from the inside.

He hadn't expected to be knocked sideways by her smile. And he didn't have the faintest clue what to do about this. Stick to being sensible—being more like his twin, in accordance with the pact they'd made—or follow his impulses?

Of course he should hold back. He and Florence barely knew each other. But being aware of that didn't stop the longing.

'You were good with Mr Walker's wife and daughter,' she said.

He shrugged off the compliment. 'Families worry, and that makes a patient even more anxious. I've always thought one of the best things you can do for a patient is to keep their families calm.'

'Good point,' she said.

'When he started getting agitated, I was beginning to think we'd have to sedate him—

which would have been horrible for him and his family.'

'Luckily it didn't come to that. And you were really good with him,' she said. She looked at him over the rim of her mug. 'So where were you before you came here?'

This was where Rob knew he needed to be careful about how much information he gave. He didn't want his past getting in the way. Didn't want to seem weak. 'Manchester,' he said. Which was true, up to a point. Just he'd been in the middle of taking a sabbatical to work abroad. 'You?'

'I trained in Leeds, then moved here just over a year ago,' she said, 'to be near my family.'

'Me, too. My parents retired near here,' he said. It was the truth; just not the whole truth, because if the appendicitis and blood poisoning hadn't happened he would still have been working for the humanitarian organisation, or by now he would've been back in Manchester and spending his spare time with the local mountain rescue team, really making a difference and using his skills. But he was glad Florence had mentioned her family. He needed to head her off. Since she'd moved back here to be close to them, it followed that she was likely to be happy to talk about them. It would be the perfect distraction. 'So your family's local?'

'My parents live in the next village—I grew up here,' she said. 'My older sister moved back here two years ago when she retired.'

Hang on. Florence looked as if she was around the same age as he was, thirty. Even if there was a ten-year gap between her and her sister, that didn't quite stack up. 'Retired?'

'Lexy's a ballerina,' Florence explained. 'She's thirty-six—a lot of ballerinas retire in their thirties, because dancing takes such a toll on their hips and knees—and anyway she doesn't want to tour with the company any more now her oldest has started school. So she's done her teaching qualification, and she's set up her own ballet school. All three of her daughters dance with her—even Darcey, the two-year-old.'

Rob noticed a hint of wistfulness along with the pride in her face when she spoke about her nieces, and wondered what was behind that.

And he noticed that Florence hadn't said anything about a husband. He couldn't help a swift glance at her left hand. There was no ring, though that didn't mean anything; she could still be in a committed relationship.

He needed to damp down that zing of attraction towards her, fast. Those huge brown eyes. The generous curve of her mouth. The way everything suddenly felt a little bit brighter when she was in the room.

'Darcey? It's an unusual name.'

'After Darcey Bussell. Lexy called her girls after famous ballerinas. Margot—the oldest—is named after Margot Fonteyn, and Anna, who's four, is named after Anna Pavlova.'

Even Rob had heard of the ballerinas. 'Got you.'

He managed to keep the conversation work-based for the rest of their break, then walked with Florence back to the department.

It was a busy afternoon and, although he hated to admit it, he was tired by the time he got home. There was a note in his letter-box saying that a parcel had been delivered next door; even before he picked it up, he had a pretty good idea who'd sent it. The person he'd done exactly the same thing for, a couple of months back; the person whose thoughts so often chimed with his.

There was a note attached:

*You are only allowed to open this if you DIDN'T overdo things on your first day.*

'Yeah, yeah, Olls,' he said with a grin, and opened it. The parcel contained a bottle of good red wine and some seriously good chocolate.

Perfect for his first evening after work.

Rob texted his twin. Thank you for the parcel. I so deserve this.

His phone rang seconds later. 'So how was your first day?' Oliver asked.

'Wonderful. It was so good to be back, Olls. To save lives—we had an arrest and we got him back. And even if it's only three days a week, it's so much better to know I'm making a difference again instead of being stuck at home.' Stuck feeling too ill even to pace about. It had been Rob's worst nightmare.

'Glad you enjoyed it. Are your colleagues nice?'

Rob thought of Florence Jacobs. 'Very.' Though he wasn't going to admit to his twin that he'd been drawn to one new colleague in particular.

'And you paced yourself?' Oliver checked.

'Stop nagging. Of course I did. I'm a bit tired, now,' Rob admitted, 'but I've got tomorrow off to recover. Working every other day is going to ease me back into things. I know it'll be a while yet before I'm ready to go full time again, but working part time is way, way better than doing nothing.'

'That all sounds a bit sensible for *you*. So you actually meant it about being more Ollie?' his twin teased.

'Yes.' Mostly. He wasn't sure if he was actually capable of putting down roots.

Though he was very aware of how impersonal his rented flat was. The one thing that Rob did envy Ollie was the way his twin always seemed able to make a place feel like a home, even on the same day he moved in. Rob was never in a place for long enough to make it feel properly like home; he was too busy chasing the next adventure, making the next difference. And even his flat in Manchester— currently rented out to a colleague—was just a place to stay between the emergency department, climbing and his overseas work.

Maybe he should try taking a few more leaves out of Ollie's book.

Tomorrow, he decided, he'd print out some of the photos on his phone and stick them in frames on the mantelpiece. That might make his flat feel less anonymous and soulless.

'I'm starving, so I'm going to say goodbye now and cook dinner,' he said.

'You mean, you're going to stick something in the microwave,' Oliver teased.

'It's perfectly nutritious. There are two portions of my five a day, and I'm having an apple afterwards.' Unlike his twin, Rob never had been big on cooking. It always felt like a waste of time where he could be doing something more active and more interesting. His rule was that if it took more than five minutes, it was off the menu. 'I'll call you tomorrow,' he said. 'Give Gemma my love. And thank you for the care package.'

'You're welcome. And you can always come here for dinner after work, if you're tired. I don't mind cooking for you.'

'That's kind,' Rob said. Though Ollie was newly loved up; given that the kidney transplant had been the thing to break his brother's engagement, the last thing Rob wanted now was to put pressure on Ollie's new relationship. Even though Rob liked Gemma very much and thought she was a million times better for Ollie than Tabby had been, and also wasn't likely to behave in the same way, he still didn't want to make things difficult. 'Oh, by the way. How's your patient with chickenpox pneumonia doing?'

'She's completely recovered,' Oliver said. 'But I don't remember telling you about that. Why do you ask?'

'One of my new colleagues remembered you bringing her in. She thought I was you.'

'Oh?' Oliver sounded intrigued.

'And I'm hungry,' Rob said, 'so I'm going.' Before he said anything about Florence Jacobs that his twin might misinterpret.

Florence walked into the kitchen, her footsteps echoing.

It was more than a year now since she'd moved back to Northumbria. More than a year since her divorce. More than two years since her world had collapsed.

And, although she'd grown up only a few miles away in the next village, this place still didn't feel like home. A single person's flat. Empty. This wasn't the life she'd planned for herself; she'd thought by now she'd have children at preschool—children who'd grow up close to their cousins, the way Florence had been close to her sister.

Instead, she was on her own. And she just didn't have the strength to try again.

She didn't regret moving back from Leeds. Being close to the family she loved, being able to see her nieces grow up—that meant the world to her. And it was nice not having anyone at work pitying her, or the whispered conversations that stopped abruptly when she walked into the staff kitchen.

She knew her colleagues in Leeds had speculated about the break-up of her marriage, and it was obvious they'd all guessed Dan's affair had been at the root of it because Florence had adored her husband. But telling them the whole truth would've been so much harder. That she and Dan had tried for a baby for three years, the tests had shown that he was the one with the fertility problem, and he'd refused flatly to adopt, foster or to go through IVF with a sperm donor. He'd refused to go to counselling, too, and he'd given her an ultimatum of a baby or him.

How ironic that now she had neither. And Dan had ended up marrying a single mum who'd given him the children he hadn't been able to have himself but had refused to give Florence: the woman he'd had an affair with. The more she thought about it, the more she realised that maybe Dan's issues hadn't been with having children; it had been having children with *her*. And just what was so wrong with her that the love of her life hadn't wanted to make a family with her?

She shook herself. 'Enough of the pity party,' she told herself crossly. Time to look on the bright side. Focus on what she did have, not what she didn't. She loved her family and lived close enough to see a lot of them; she had a job she adored; and she had good friends who looked out for her. She was lucky.

Though she knew exactly what had unsettled her today.

Robert Langley.

Her new colleague was charming, great with patients, and he treated all staff as equally important—whatever their position on the ward. He thought on his feet, so he was good to work with. He was more than easy on the eye.

And maybe that was the problem.

Because in some ways he reminded her of Dan, when they'd first got together. Dan, who was urbane and charming and got on well with everyone. Dan, who she'd thought she'd be with for ever: until he'd changed the goalposts and broken her heart in the process.

Rob hadn't mentioned having a partner or children, and she'd got the impression that there was something a little remote about him. As if that charm was a barrier to stop people seeing who he really was, behind it.

'Or maybe you're overthinking things and being incredibly unfair to your new colleague, Florence Jacobs,' she said out loud.

To get her balance back, she needed to go

for a run and get the endorphins flowing, and have dinner. And until then she wasn't going to allow herself to think about Robert Langley.

# CHAPTER TWO

TWO DAYS LATER, Rob was in Minors. In the middle of the morning, a man came in after a car accident where he'd been rear-ended while waiting in a queue of traffic. He rolled his eyes at his wife. 'I'm sorry we're wasting your time, Doctor. I'm only here because my wife won't stop fussing.'

'Actually,' Rob said, 'your wife has a point. Even though modern cars have good crumple zones, the impact might have affected you more than you think.'

'And he was slurring his words earlier,' his wife said. 'When he rang me I couldn't understand a word he said.'

'Because I was standing on the side of the road waiting for the tow truck and I was *cold*,' her husband said crossly, 'not because I had an undiagnosed bleed to my brain or something. You watch too many hospital dramas,

Mags. They're not going to need to airlift me somewhere.'

Rob had to hide a smile. 'OK. Did the airbag go off?'

'No. I was sitting in a queue of traffic waiting to turn right when the guy rammed into me. I had my lights on and my indicator going, but he said he didn't see me. Idiot. He wasn't looking where he was going.'

'The car's likely to be written off,' his wife said, 'so it was quite an impact.'

'Let me check you over,' Rob said. He checked his patient's neck and head, got him to follow a moving finger with his eye, then checked his back. 'Your muscles are pretty tight from the impact, so you're going to be sore for a week or so. You need good painkillers and rest—and I *mean* rest. Plus it'll help you to do some gentle stretching.'

'See? You made a fuss about nothing,' the man said to his wife.

'No, it was a good call,' Rob said. 'Until the beginning of this year, I would've been on your side. Now I know better.'

The man looked curious. 'What made you change your mind?'

'A burst appendix,' Rob said. 'I was working abroad and I assumed my stomach pains were just because I wasn't used to the food or water. And me a doctor. You'd think I'd know better.' He gave a rueful smile. 'So I've learned not to ignore things any more. The quicker you get something checked out, the easier it is to pick up a problem and get it sorted before it turns into something serious.'

'Got you,' the man said.

'You might find your back feels more painful over the next couple of days. If it feels worse in a week's time, come back or see your GP to get checked over—and none of the stiff upper lip stuff, OK? Because all that'll do is mean your recovery will be longer.'

'OK,' the patient said.

Rob gave his patient a prescription for painkillers—stronger ones than were available to buy over the counter at a pharmacy or supermarket. 'There's a week's worth. Take two with food, maximum eight in twenty-four hours, and if they're not touching the pain then come back.'

When it was time for his break, he headed for the staff kitchen. Florence was there, and his heart did a weird little flip. Rob had to remind himself that it wasn't a good idea to act on the attraction he felt towards her.

'Kettle's hot,' she said.

'Cheers.' He put a couple of spoons of instant coffee into a mug and added boiling water to dissolve it, then enough cold water so he could start drinking it. 'How was your morning?'

'I had a whole run of Colles' fractures— and it's not even icy this morning,' she said.

'Yeah, it goes like that sometimes.'

She paused. 'So you had a burst appendix at the beginning of the year?'

He looked at her, surprised. 'Hospital gossip travels fast here.'

'No. I was in the cubicle next door to your patient who'd been rear-ended, so I heard what you said. Though I haven't repeated it to anyone else.'

'Thank you.' He gave her what he hoped was a casual smile. 'It wasn't my finest moment. Helping with the aftermath of an earthquake and ending up needing treatment myself.' He wasn't quite ready to admit how serious it had got after the burst appendix. The blood poisoning. The dialysis. The horror of being *stuck* when he was desperate to be on the move again.

'Good advice you gave your patient, though.'

'It's not so easy to follow advice if you have a Y chromosome,' he deadpanned.

She laughed. 'At least you're honest about it.' She smiled at him, and again his heart did that little flip. Her mouth was beautiful. He had difficulty stopping himself reaching out to trace the lower curve with his forefinger. Which was crazy. He hadn't felt this kind of unstoppable attraction towards someone in years—not since he was twenty-four, in his first job after graduating, and fallen for a fellow medic.

Except Janine had had a five-year plan that included marriage, a mortgage and children; and that was completely incompatible with Rob's own plans to travel the world. It had ended in tears, and Rob had never really forgiven himself for not being what she needed and for hurting her. It was why he made sure all his girlfriends knew he didn't do serious: so he'd never hurt anyone again.

This pull he felt towards Florence unnerved him. Why now? Why her? What the hell was going on in his head? Equally pretty women had crossed his path in the last few months, so it wasn't that he'd been starved of female company—even though he hadn't been well enough to take things further.

What was so special about Florence Jacobs?

Before he could analyse it further, she said, 'Has anyone mentioned the department Christmas dinner to you? It's Friday next week, but we've still got a day or two to finalise numbers, so I'm pretty sure we can squeeze you in if you want.'

'Christmas dinner?' Right now it was the last week of September. He stared at her in surprise. 'In October?'

'Which is the closest to Christmas we'd dare to organise it. You know what it's like in November and December. The department's so busy that nobody would be actually able to go,' she pointed out.

'True,' he said. And he knew Ollie would nag him to accept the invitation. Going for the meal would be a good way of getting to know his new team, even though he was only going to be here for three months. Gone just after Christmas. 'Thanks. I'm not on duty next Friday, so I'd like to go. Do you need a deposit or the full payment?'

'I'm guessing that it's the whole lot, as Shobu collected the rest of the money and the menu choices from everyone last week,' she said. 'Oh—and partners are welcome, too.'

'No partner. Just me,' he said.

He was single?

There was absolutely no reason for her pulse to kick up a notch.

Robert Langley was simply her new colleague, and anyway Florence wasn't interested

in another relationship—not after the way her
marriage had collapsed. She wasn't risking
her heart again. And there was no reason to
think that Rob was attracted to her, either.
'OK. Have a word with Shobu,' she said.

'I will. Oh, and I meant to tell you—your
chickenpox pneumonia lady is doing just fine.'
He smiled. 'I asked my brother when I spoke
to him, the other night.'

'That's good to know.' And it warmed her
that he'd bothered to ask. That he'd remembered.

Florence spent the next week and a half telling herself that Robert Langley was just one
of her colleagues and kept him at a friendly
but professional distance...until she walked
into the hotel where the department's Christmas meal was being held.

Shobu had obviously told him that they all
dressed up: the dress code for their Christmas
party was dinner jackets and cocktail dresses.
Florence hadn't been prepared for just how
amazing Rob looked in a tuxedo and bow
tie instead of his white coat. Not a black tie,
though; when she got closer, she discovered
it was black with a dark grey paisley pattern.
Incredibly stylish. Incredibly sexy. He still had

that designer stubble that made her want to touch him.

And she needed to get a grip.

'Didn't fancy a polka dot red tie, then?' she said, aiming for teasing and hoping he wouldn't guess how attractive she found him.

'I thought red might be a tiny bit too showy-offy,' he said. 'You look amazing, by the way.'

'Thank you.' She'd borrowed a dress from Lexy: a simple black shift dress that came down to just above her knee and had a boat neck. She wore a single strand of pearls and matching earrings—also Lexy's—and her sister had insisted on doing her make-up, while her nieces all told her she looked like a princess. 'Though it's borrowed finery. I'm more one for scrubs or a white coat.'

'Still lovely,' he said.

He was being polite, she told herself. There was no reason to feel that flush of pleasure. No reason to feel a little tingle at the ends of her fingers. No reason for her breath to catch.

The breath-catching feeling got worse during the meal, because she was sitting next to Rob. And somehow they ended up brushing hands; every time it happened, her pulse rate went up another notch.

She needed to get things back on an even keel. Find a safe subject.

But, as she turned to him to say something innocuous about how lovely the food was, she caught his eye.

Oh, help.

Up this close, she could see how gorgeous his eyes were. How long his lashes were. How beautiful the shape of his mouth was.

Thinking about his mouth was a bad idea. Because the next step from that was thinking about how that beautiful mouth might feel against her skin. And her kissing days were over. She wasn't going to let herself be vulnerable again.

'Lovely food, isn't it?' she asked brightly, hoping nobody could hear the note of panic in her voice—and hoping even more that nobody would guess what was behind it. Especially Rob.

'Very nice,' he agreed.

He shuffled slightly in his seat, and the chairs were close enough together that his leg pressed briefly against hers. Even through the material of his trousers, she could feel the warmth of his skin, and it made her want to press against him.

'So there's dancing after this?' he asked.

*Dancing.* Up close and personal…

No.

Her scrambled brain needed to find an answer before he wondered why she wasn't saying a word.

'They'll play all the Christmas hits, and everyone will be jumping about and singing their heads off,' she said. Which was safe dancing. Enjoying yourself with your friends and colleagues. Not dangerous dancing, one on one.

'With your sister being a ballerina, does that mean you like dancing?'

She'd loved it. And Dan had been an excellent dancer. It was one of the reasons she'd fallen for him in the first place: dancing with Dan had been like floating on air.

They hadn't danced together for a good year before he'd left her. And she hadn't had a clue that he'd been dancing with someone else.

Not wanting to let the old hurts spoil tonight—or let herself wonder what it would be like to dance with Rob—she deliberately misinterpreted his question so he wouldn't take it as an invitation to ask her to dance. 'Follow in her footsteps? No. I went to ballet lessons when I was five, for about a term, but it wasn't for me. I loved the music, I loved watching Lexy dance at home—and dancing with her—but I wasn't like her. I didn't want to put in the hours and hours of practice, the way she did.'

For a second, there was a glint in his eyes, as if he recognised the subterfuge: stick to a safe, neutral topic.

And then how ridiculous was it that she felt almost disappointed when he did precisely that and asked, 'What made you decide to be a doctor?'

'I wanted to do something where I'd help people,' she said, 'and when I did my rotation in the Emergency Department it made me realise that was where I wanted to be.' Since he'd opted for the safe topic, it would only be polite to ask him the same. 'What about you?'

He grinned. 'Ah, now. When I was thirteen, I flirted with the idea of being a rock star.'

Florence could just imagine it; and she could all too clearly imagine Rob on stage. Whatever role he'd taken in the band, even if he'd been stuck at the back behind a drum kit, he would've drawn all the attention. Just as he was holding her attention now. Her mouth felt as if it was glued to the roof of her mouth. Rob as a rock star... She shook herself mentally and strove for a note of friendly teasing. 'So how much of a flirtation was it? You thought about doing it and mimed a bit, or do you actually play something?'

'Oh, I had a proper band—me, my brother and a friend.' He laughed. 'I was going to be the lead guitarist and singer, Ollie did the bass and harmonies, and our mate Micky was the drummer. We used to practise in our garage.' He laughed even more. 'Weirdly, the whole street seemed to go out within five minutes of us turning our amps on.'

'You were that good?' she teased.

'We were terrible. And I mean *really* terrible. I'm not sure who was most relieved when we stopped, our parents or our neighbours.'

His eyes crinkled at the corners when he laughed. That gorgeous, gorgeous blue. It made her stomach swoop just to look at him.

He must know the effect he had on women. Yet he hadn't claimed that his band was brilliant and he could've been a pop star if he'd wanted to. He'd laughed about his own hopelessness. There was no posturing, no side to him. She liked that. She liked *him*. And that was enough to tip her into confessing, 'I never wanted to be in a band, but Lexy and I used to sing into hairbrushes in the kitchen on a Sunday morning.'

'So you can sing?' He looked interested.

'I can just about hold a tune,' she said, 'but it's more the sort of thing I do in the car with Mum, or with Lexy and the girls. There's no way you'd ever get me up at the mic at a karaoke night.'

'Got you.'

'So, when you gave up the idea of being a rock star, what made you decide on medicine?' she asked.

'I fell in love with climbing,' he said, 'and I joined the local mountain rescue team. And it was a fairly easy step from learning first aid for mountain rescue to wanting to do full-on emergency medicine.' He smiled. 'I always found it a bit hard to sit still, as a kid, so I like the pace in the department. It suits me.'

And she found herself wondering what else would suit him. What else he liked. What made him tick.

Which was crazy. She didn't want to get involved with anyone, outside friendship. So why did Robert Langley snag her attention like this? Why couldn't she take her eyes off him? Why was she aware of every tiny shift in his body and every time his hand accidentally brushed against hers?

Thankfully the Head of Department saved her from blurting out something stupid by tapping a spoon against his glass and then doing the usual speech before giving out the 'secret Santa' presents. She wondered whose name Rob been given; this late on, she guessed that Shobu had probably swapped names with him.

The gifts were the usual mix of novelty

socks, Christmas tree decorations for beards, good chocolate, mugs with rude slogans and silly games. Florence ended up with a gorgeous scented candle; Rob was given socks sporting polar bears wearing Santa hats.

And then the dancing started.

Rob had been very aware of Florence all through dinner. Every time his hand had brushed against hers, every time one of them had shifted in their chairs and accidentally pressed a leg against the other's, it had increased his awareness of her. The dress she was wearing made him think even more of Audrey Hepburn. And he really wanted to dance with her. Hold her close. Sway with her to sweet, soft music.

The sensible side of him knew that he should jam a lid on that attraction before it spilled over. Even though he knew from general chat in the staff kitchen that Florence was single, it didn't mean that she was looking for a relationship; though, from the way her gorgeous brown eyes had widened at him, he was pretty sure that she'd felt that same simmering awareness of him during dinner.

He ought to keep his distance. Dance with her in a group. Keep it all light and friendly and totally above board.

Except he was finding her irresistible.

He danced with two of the nurses, one of the other doctors and two of the support staff; all the while, he knew exactly where Florence was on the dance floor, even when his back was to her. For pity's sake. He wasn't looking for a partner. He wanted to concentrate on getting fully fit again so he could go back to his old life—or, at least, as much of it as possible. Climbing. Things that his past girlfriends had lost patience with—which was another of the reasons why his relationships never lasted. And why was he thinking about relationships now? This was ridiculous.

But he couldn't take his eyes off Florence. *The way she moved.*

Florence had been dancing all evening. Exactly the fun, safe dancing she'd intended to enjoy. But all the while she'd been very aware of exactly where Rob was on the dance floor. He'd admitted to being a terrible singer, but he was a good dancer. He paid attention to the way his partner moved. And she noticed that he danced with every single woman in their group, smiling and charming them: though in a nice way, not a sleazy way. He was inclusive, making sure that everyone had a good time.

Rob Langley was good with people.

And he was more than easy on the eye.

And he was single…

She shook herself. Not happening. Temporary colleagues only, she reminded herself. No complications, no disappointments, no heartbreak. She was done with having her heart broken and her dreams trampled into dust.

She smiled. Chatted to her colleagues. Danced. Smiled a bit more.

And then, at the end of the song, she felt as if she was tingling all over.

Rob was there.

Right next to her.

'Dr Jacobs. Would you care to dance?' he asked.

How could she possible resist? Though she made an attempt at a casual, 'Sure.'

Except this *would* have to be the song where the lights dimmed and everything slowed right down. The song where they ended up swaying close.

Before, she'd been chatting and laughing during a dance with a group of people.

Now, she was in his arms. Holding him close. Close enough to feel the warmth of his skin through his shirt, the warmth of his hand against her back.

Florence could hardly breathe.

Despite her high heels, she wasn't quite tall

enough to dance cheek to cheek with him, but his nearness made her feel almost dizzy. How long had it been since she'd danced with someone like this? Even Dan…they hadn't danced together for years. They'd been too busy fighting about making babies—or, rather, *not* making them.

And this time Rob wasn't chatting about his teenage years and asking her about her family. He was holding her close enough for her to be able to feel the warmth of his body, the beat of his heart.

She pulled back slightly and risked glancing up at him. The intensity of his gaze practically seared her.

So did this mean he felt the same way that she did? As if the whole of the dance floor had just melted away, all the people and the music vanished into space, and there was just the two of them in the room? Did he, too, feel this sweet, crazy longing?

Maybe the questions showed in her eyes, because he drew her closer. Stooped a little more, so they were actually dancing cheek to cheek. And then she felt the touch of his lips at the corner of her mouth. Like gossamer. No pressure, no demands: just light and sweet and so very tempting.

Only a kiss. One little, tiny kiss.

What would be the harm in following his lead and kissing him back?

Not giving her common sense the chance to talk her out of it, she turned her face slightly so her lips brushed against his, and it sent a tingle through her whole body: as if every vein, every nerve-ending, had suddenly lit up. It almost knocked her off balance; except his arms were round her, holding her safely so she didn't fall, guiding her round the dance floor.

This wasn't meant to be happening.

For pity's sake. They were in a public place. Among lots of people they both worked with. It wasn't appropriate to start snogging his face off, as if they were teenagers.

Except then he kissed her. Still light, still gentle. And Florence couldn't think straight any more after that.

She was aware that the song had changed but the tempo hadn't. If she had any sense, she'd make herself take a step backwards and suggest he dance with someone else. Except she couldn't. She wanted his arms wrapped round her and hers round him, cocooning them both. She wanted to feel his heart beating in time with her own.

Even when the music changed tempo again and she managed to back away enough so that they both danced with other people, she was still so aware of Rob and how it had felt to kiss him. It set little tingles running all the way through her, and she was shocked to realise that it was desire.

It had been so long since she'd felt like that about anyone. Since she'd allowed herself to feel like that about anyone, because memories of the bitterness with Dan had held her back. And it threw her, to the point where she had no idea what to do about it.

Rob hadn't set out intentionally to kiss Florence. It had just happened. But it had shaken him. He couldn't remember the last time he'd felt like this: like a teenager who finally summoned up the courage to risk being knocked back by the girl he'd liked for ages and kissing her.

Florence hadn't knocked him back.

And he hadn't known her for ages, just for a couple of weeks.

He needed to be sensible. Like his twin. He remembered the deal they'd made. *Be more Ollie.* What would Oliver do now? He'd dance with his colleagues and his colleagues' partners, he'd make small talk, and he'd smile a lot. OK. It was a plan. A good plan. Rob followed it to the letter.

But, all the while, he was so aware of exactly where Florence was in the room. Moth to a flame, magnet, any cliché you wanted to pick: it was a mash-up of all of them. The end result was the same. There was a definite connection between them, and he wanted to explore it and find out what it meant. At the same time, he wanted to back off. And he wasn't used to being confused like this. He worked in emergency medicine, and all his favourite pastimes needed the same ability he needed at work: to be able to assess a situation and make a fast, informed decision. No dithering.

So why was he dithering now? Why was he such a mess?

Rob had planned to be sensible and say a cheerful goodnight to Florence at the end of the evening, just as he had with his other colleagues, but what came out of his mouth was something different. 'Do you have to rush off, or could you stay and have a drink with me?'

'The hotel's closing,' she said, her gorgeous brown eyes looking huge in the low light.

'Not for residents.'

She looked surprised. 'You're staying here tonight?'

'Yes.' It had been his back-up plan so, if the bone-deep tiredness that still occasionally hit him kicked in, he wouldn't have to worry about getting back to his rented flat. Not that he was going to tell her about any of that. 'Come and have a drink with me at the bar,' he said.

'A nightcap?'

Would she stay? Or would she back off? He wanted her to stay; but at the same time he wasn't used to reacting to someone like this. And his mouth felt so dry he couldn't speak. He just nodded.

'All right. I'll have a glass of wine with you, on condition I buy the drinks.'

Funny how that made him feel like punching the air. Not that he'd be stupid enough to do that in front of her. Relief loosened his tongue again. 'I don't think they'll let you pay. The bar is for residents only,' he said with a smile. 'Though you can buy me a coffee some time next week instead, if it makes you feel better.'

What?

Why had he said that, as if he was setting up a date?

But she didn't run a mile. She just nodded. 'It's a deal.'

He found them a table in a quiet corner of the bar, checked what she wanted to drink, and bought them both a glass of dry white wine. And, while they chatted, he found himself watching her while she sipped her wine. Remembering how that mouth had felt against his, the warmth and the pressure and the sweetness. He wanted it to happen all over again. Wanted to kiss her back. Wanted to feel her melt into him.

When he caught her eye, she blushed. So was she thinking the same? Was she remembering how it had felt to kiss him? Did she want more?

She put her glass down. 'I should go.'

That would be sensible. But before he could stop himself, he said, 'Though there's another option.' His pulse kicked up a notch at the very thought of it, making him catch his breath and knocking all his common sense out of his head. 'You could stay.'

'Stay.'

She'd clearly just remembered that he had a room. Somewhere they could be private. Somewhere they could explore what was happening between them.

He could see the argument warring in her expression—should she stay, or should she go? What was holding her back? Did she think it would be difficult between them at work?

'If it makes a difference,' he said, 'this would be just between you and me, until we're both sure where this is going.'

There was a long, long pause.

Finally, she asked, 'And if I decide to stay?' There was the tiniest, tiniest crack in her voice.

Did she feel as nervous as he did?

He wanted to reassure her, yet at the same time he needed to let her know that he wanted her. 'I don't know,' he said. 'I wasn't planning this.' It was crazy. He was used to making fast decisions—*good* decisions—but they were judgements based on past experience.

This felt new. Like a step into the unknown. And it made him catch his breath.

Or maybe the admission was the reassurance she needed: that he felt as much at sixes and sevens as she did. Because then she smiled. 'Yes.'

One little word.

And it made all the difference.

He stood up in silence and stretched his hand out to her. She stood up, took his hand, and walked to the lift with him.

The lift was surprisingly small, only just big enough for both of them to fit. Once the doors had closed behind them, Rob cupped her face gently in his hands and brushed his mouth lightly against hers.

She shivered when he broke the kiss.

'It wasn't supposed to happen like this,' he

said softly, 'but life throws curveballs as well as good things. And nowadays I'm minded to catch the good things.'

'Me, too,' she said, and the look on her face told him she'd had some hard curveballs in the past.

He took her hand as they left the lift and kept holding it all the way down the corridor.

Please don't let the card key fail him and break the understanding between them. Please let them stay in this glorious, shiny bubble. Just the two of them and this shimmery feeling.

To his relief, his card key worked first time. He opened the door, stood aside to let her go into the room first, then slid the card into the slot by the light.

The lamp in the corner of the room was the only one lit, and she looked suddenly nervous as she perched on the edge of the chair. Yeah. He knew how that felt.

'You can change your mind,' he reassured her quietly. 'I can call you a taxi. There's no pressure to do anything you don't want to do, Florence.'

Giving her the choice seemed to decide her. 'Or there's another option,' she said, her voice husky.

His heart skipped another beat. 'What might that be?'

She stood up, closed the gap between them and kissed him.

It felt as if fireworks were going off in his head, splinters of gold and silver and starlight. As if he'd come back to life again after all these months of being stuck. She didn't see him as a patient; she saw him as a man. She wanted him as much as he wanted her. And this was going to happen.

When he broke the kiss, he turned her round and undid the zip of her dress, kissing his way down her spine as he did so.

She gave a little wriggle. He wasn't sure if it was pleasure or awkwardness, so he erred on the side of caution and turned her back round to face him. 'Everything all right?' he checked.

'Yes.'

'Good.' He kissed her lightly, then eased the dress over her shoulders and let it pool on the floor.

'You're beautiful,' he whispered, and traced the lacy edge of her bra with one finger.

She moistened her lower lip with the tip of her tongue, and his pulse speeded up.

'You're fully dressed. I think we need to even up the balance,' she said.

'I'm in your hands,' he said.

She struggled a bit with his bow tie, but finally managed it. His shirt was next, and he found breathing difficult as she undid each button, her fingers brushing against his skin and sending little shocks of pleasure across his nerve-ends.

Waiting wasn't something he was good at; but if he rushed her now he knew she'd back away and he'd never have another chance. So he let her set the pace, let her fingers explore the breadth of his shoulders, the muscles of his back. Every stroke, every touch drove him crazy with need. He was practically quivering when she stopped. 'Florence?'

Please don't let her call a halt. He took her hand, lifted it to his mouth, and kissed each fingertip in turn. 'I'm trying to let you set the pace,' he said. 'But my self-control is shredding by the second. I'm not sure how much longer I can hold out.'

Oh, the things that rueful smile did to her insides.

Rob Langley was charming, and he knew it.

But he was also sexy as hell, and Florence wanted him. The way she'd felt when he'd danced with her—it had been a long, long time since she'd felt like that. For a couple of years before her marriage had turned bad, if she was honest about it. And she wanted to feel like that again. Come back out of the cold loneliness of her life. Let him heat her blood to boiling point.

He'd given her the control.

Time to make it snap.

She stood on tiptoe and kissed him.

Things went a bit fuzzy after that. The next thing Florence knew, they were lying on the bed together, both naked. She had absolutely no idea who had removed whose clothes and when. And it wasn't because she'd drunk too much wine: it was Rob's touch that made everything else feel irrelevant. Rob was kneeling between her thighs and kissing his way down her body, nuzzling the hollows of her collar bones, working his way downwards to tease each nipple in turn, then kissing his way down over her abdomen.

All Florence could think of was the way he made her feel. The warmth spreading through her as he stroked her skin, teased her with his mouth and his hands until she was quivering and nearly hyperventilating with need. She wanted him so much, it made her head spin.

Her climax shimmered through her unexpectedly. She'd almost forgotten what it felt like, that rush of pleasure bubbling through her.

'OK?' he asked.

'Very OK.' She couldn't help grinning.

He grinned back. 'Good. I wanted the first time to be for you.'

An unselfish lover. Something Dan hadn't been when their marriage had been exploding. Sex had been more like fighting. The memory made her catch her breath; but it wouldn't be fair to dump this on Rob now. So she made herself smile as if nothing was wrong.

The brittleness must've shown, though, because he kissed her very gently—reassuring, not demanding. 'You can still change your mind.'

'No, it's...complicated,' she said.

'There's someone else?'

She shook her head. 'I wouldn't do that. Just...a bit of baggage. Unwanted baggage. Ignore it.'

'Better than that. I'll try to make you forget it,' he said softly. He kissed her again, and aroused her with his hands and his mouth until she was quivering with need; it shocked her how desperately she wanted this. He ripped open the foil packet, slid on the condom, knelt between her thighs and eased into her. He waited for her to adjust to the feel of him inside her, and then he began to move.

The waves of pleasure built again and she

wrapped her legs round him, drawing him deeper.

This time, they hit the peak at the same time, and they held each other tightly until the little aftershocks had died away.

'Better deal with the condom,' he said, gently disentangling himself, and headed for the en suite bathroom.

Was this her cue to leave?

It had been so long since she'd done anything like this. She couldn't remember what the etiquette was. Did she get dressed and leave? Or did she stay?

She was still trying to work her way through the dilemma when he came back from the bathroom. And that was when she noticed the scar on his lower abdomen. It was in the same place as she'd expect to see a scar from an appendectomy, but the colour of the skin made the scar look newer than he'd said it was.

Clearly he realised what she was seeing, because he grimaced. 'Sorry. I should've put a towel round me or something.'

She shook her head. 'It's not that. It looks… new.'

He could trust her—or he could back away.

He took a deep breath while he thought

about it, then decided. 'OK. Short version: I had a kidney transplant back in June. My consultant cleared me to go back to work part time, so I'm easing myself back into things. That's why I'm only doing three days a week on the ward.'

Her eyes narrowed. 'A kidney transplant is a pretty major thing.'

He sighed. 'I know. The head of department knows about it but we agreed to keep it between us. I don't want people thinking I'm weak or I can't do my job.'

'Why would they think that?'

'Because...' He sighed. 'Because that's how I've felt for months, being unable to do anything I'd normally do. I've hated people treating me as if I'm fragile. That's not who I am.'

'Definitely not a delicate little flower,' she agreed.

'Are you...?' She was. That little glimmer in her eyes. She was *teasing* him. All the fight went out of him. He gave her a rueful smile. 'No. Though I'm kind of behaving like one. It's just...you've seen me as *me*. I don't want that to change.'

'I'm not going to judge you,' she said. 'It sounds to as me as if you're already doing quite enough of that for yourself.'

'Maybe,' he admitted. 'It's messed with my head, not being able to do what I've always done. Feeling as if I've been stuffed into a box that gets smaller every day.'

'Tell me,' she said softly. 'It isn't going any further than me.'

'I've already worked out for myself that you're not a gossip.'

'Thank you,' she said. 'Just for the record, I didn't tell anyone what I heard you say about your appendix.'

'Thank you.' He blew out a breath. 'I was volunteering for a humanitarian aid organisation, helping out after an earthquake. I have skills that can be useful and I like working in challenging situations. I'd been feeling a bit rough, but I put that down to a change in water and food.' He shrugged. 'It turned out it was my appendix, which then ruptured. I ended up with severe blood poisoning and it wiped out my kidneys. I was on dialysis for a while.' And he'd felt every second dragging by, slower than a glacier scraping across a valley. 'I needed a transplant. Ollie—my brother—was a live donor and gave me one of his kidneys.'

'That's an amazing thing to do for someone,' she said.

'I know. He's an amazing man.' He looked at her. 'And I appreciate you listening.'

'No problem.' She looked at him. 'So what now?'

'Now I've completely ruined the mood?'

'I was the one who brought up the subject,' she said. 'So you can't take the entire blame.'

'I guess,' he said wryly. 'I can call you a taxi, if you'd like. Or…' He took a deep breath. 'Or you can stay. Fall asleep with me. Let go and forget the world, just for a little while. Just you and me. No baggage.'

It was tempting.

So very, very tempting.

After all, what did she have to go back to? An empty flat that still didn't feel like home. Or she could stay here, curl up in the arms of the man who'd just made her feel so amazing. Forget everything that had made her miserable in the last few years. Enjoy this warmth and closeness, just for a while. No promises, no complications.

The decision was easy.

'I'll stay,' she said.

He smiled, and helped her tidy up their clothes, before taking her hand and drawing her back to bed. He lay on his back, and she curled into him, resting her head on his shoulder and letting her fingers entwine loosely with his.

She'd worry about tomorrow later.

Tonight, she'd just *be*.

# CHAPTER THREE

THE NEXT MORNING, Florence woke, feeling warm and comfortable. It took a moment for her to realise she wasn't in her own bed. And another to realise that a body was cuddled round hers, an arm wrapped round her and keeping her against him. And another to remember the night before: dancing with Rob, kissing him, making love...

Which meant she'd just made her life complicated.

They hadn't actually made any promises to each other.

But how was she going to face him this morning?

She didn't want another relationship. After the misery of the way her marriage had ended, she didn't want to risk her heart ever again. Last night, she'd given in to temptation—and the possibilities filled her with panic.

Would Rob see this as the start of something? Last night, he'd said about forgetting the world for a while. No baggage. They'd agreed on one night: but how would he see things this morning?

Even though she knew they really needed to talk about this, the whole thing scared her stupid. If he did want it to be the start of something, she wasn't sure she could face the risk of it all going wrong, just as it had with Dan. She'd be setting herself up for rejection—and she'd already faced enough of that with Dan. She didn't want to be the one who wasn't good enough, all over again.

Plus there was the fact he'd made it clear he was only here temporarily. What was the point of starting something, letting herself fall for him, only for him to leave?

Whatever way she looked at this, it was going to end up with her being the one left. Again. She couldn't see any alternatives.

And even if her fears were all baseless—even if Rob did want a relationship, even if he changed his mind and stayed here, even if she could be brave enough to take the chance—what he'd told her last night made it clear that he was the last person she should let herself fall for. He'd had a kidney transplant. Which meant that, even though his brother was the donor of the kidney, he'd need to take immunosuppressant drugs to stop his body rejecting the new kidney. As a doctor, Florence knew that immunosuppressant drugs affected fertility. So being with Rob would put her back in exactly the same position as she'd been with Dan: with her partner unable to have children without medical intervention. And who was to say he wanted children anyway?

She couldn't handle the infertility issue again.

So it would be better to leave right now. Call a halt to this, before either of them could get any more deeply involved. She'd have to regard last night as nothing more than a fling— a fling that had made her feel amazing, but it wasn't to be repeated so she needed to stuff her emotions and all the longing back in the box where they belonged. And she'd have to keep things strictly professional between them for the rest of his temporary stay in their department.

His breathing appeared to be deep and even. What were the chances of her being able to move his arm away from her, wriggle out of bed, get dressed and leave without him waking? she wondered.

Probably slender, but she was going to try.

Even though she knew it was cowardly and a bit mean. At least it might save them both a bit of embarrassment. She'd text him later to apologise.

Carefully, she slid her fingers under his arm and moved it upwards.

He responded by murmuring and drawing her closer.

Oh, help. So there was no way out of this.

OK. She'd try another approach. Be brisk and efficient. Wake him, tell him she needed to leave—without making any excuses—and ask him to look away while she dressed at the speed of light.

She took a deep breath, moved his arm away and slid to the side of the bed. 'Rob. *Rob.*'

He was awake instantly. 'Florence?'

'Sorry. I need to go.'

She climbed out of bed. Then she made the mistake of looking at him. Those gorgeous blue eyes. The stubble that had made her want to touch his face. The sensual curve of his mouth.

It made her remember how he'd made her feel last night. He'd been generous, focusing on her pleasure. Even the first time had been way better than a first time should've been: no awkwardness or embarrassment, just exploring and delighting in their discoveries. They'd made love twice more in the night, and their bodies had been so in tune...

She needed to go. Now. Before she compounded her mistake, lost herself in Rob's arms again, and started to want things she couldn't have.

'Sorry,' she mumbled.

His hair was too short to be rumpled, but somehow he still managed to look all rumpled and sexy. And she was so tempted to forget all the worries spiralling in her head and climb back into bed with him.

'Why don't you stay for breakfast?' he said. 'We can order room service. Then I'll give you a lift home.'

For a second Florence could imagine it: sharing coffee with him, stealing bits of croissant from each other's plates, poring over the weekend papers and doing the crossword together...

Domestic and lovely—everything she missed from the best part of her marriage, and everything she couldn't let herself wish for again.

'Sorry. I can't. I'll get a taxi. Would you mind...um...?' Her face heated. Considering how intimate they'd been last night, asking him to avert his gaze while she dressed would make her sound like a teenager, not a sensible thirty-two-year-old.

To her relief, he didn't make her ask out loud. He just said, 'Sure,' and closed his eyes.

'Thank you.' She retrieved her clothing and dressed swiftly. As soon as she got home, she'd shower and brush her teeth and change her clothes, but for now she was going to have to brazen it out. 'I...um—I guess I'll see you at work.'

'Yeah.' His eyes were still closed, and his expression was completely unreadable.

This was one of the most awkward and embarrassing mornings she could ever remember. She didn't have a clue what to say to him—and telling him about Dan would make her feel pathetic and whiny. She was an adult who should've got over the betrayal by now. And none of this was Rob's fault. But she just couldn't explain how she felt. The words stuck in her throat.

Wanting to get out of the situation as fast as possible, she headed for the door. 'Thanks for...' Her manners deserted her: how could she possibly thank him for sex? Squirming, knowing she was behaving badly but unable to stop herself, she fled.

Thankfully she managed to get a taxi almost immediately.

Home, she thought. Home, for a hot shower, and wash some common sense back into her head.

Because she and Rob were going to have to work together for the next couple of months, and their patients had to come first. There wasn't room for embarrassment and awkwardness. She'd have to find a way of fixing this.

But she needed a shower and mug of disgustingly strong coffee before she could even start to think how to do that.

It was the worst 'morning after' Rob could ever remember.

Last night, Florence Jacobs had been soft and warm and gorgeous. He thought the sex had been good for both of them. She'd stayed; she'd slept in his arms; and while he'd been sliding into sleep he'd planned to ask her to stay for breakfast in the morning, and then suggest that maybe they could do something together—either today if she wasn't busy, or the next time they both had a day off if she already had other plans. Maybe a walk on the beach or a pub lunch: time to get to know each other without any pressure. She was the first woman in a long while he'd wanted to get to know better.

This morning, if she'd been able to get out

of bed without waking him, he was pretty sure he would've woken to find she'd vanished without even a note. As it was, she hadn't been able to get dressed and leave quickly enough.

What had gone wrong?

The more he thought about it, the more mystified he was. He was pretty sure he hadn't done anything to hurt her or upset her, but she'd made it very clear she didn't want to get to know him better. That, for her, last night was a one-off.

Maybe it was something to do with the baggage she'd mentioned last night rather than something he'd done.

But now he was beginning to realise how quite a few of his girlfriends had felt— because he was usually the one who left. The one who didn't commit. And he'd probably been fooling himself when he'd thought they'd stayed friends: because being the one who was rejected really wasn't a nice feeling. It was the first time Rob had ever felt that way, and he didn't like it. The whole thing made him feel cross with himself for wanting something he couldn't have, and ashamed of the way he'd treated his exes.

Somehow he and Florence were going to have to find a way to rewind to their professional relationship, leave the embarrassment behind and focus on their patients.

Except now he knew what it was like to kiss her. How it felt to have her skin sliding against his. The expression in her eyes when she climaxed.

He wanted more.

But she clearly didn't.

'Get a grip,' he told himself, and headed for the bathroom. A cold shower would sort his head out. And then he'd work out a plan to repair the mess he'd made.

A shower and a mug of coffee didn't make things better. Florence was completely out of sorts. Even sewing, her favourite hobby, didn't absorb her the way it usually did; instead of losing herself and her worries in the rhythm, she found herself stopping and unpicking her work. In the end, she gave up and texted her sister.

Can I come over for coffee? Xx

The reply was instant:

Course you can. xx

Lexy greeted her at the door with a big hug, then took a step back and frowned before ushering Florence into the kitchen. 'What's happened? I expected you to be buzzing after last night. You love departmental nights out. Especially when there's dancing.'

'It was fine,' Florence fibbed.

'Just "fine"?' Lexy gave her a sidelong look, then put a mug of coffee and a chocolate muffin in front of her. 'Max has taken the girls to get some bread for lunch, so they'll probably feed the ducks on the way home. We have half an hour. Talk.'

'There's nothing to say.'

Lexy folded her arms and stared at Florence.

'Don't give me your scary ballet teacher look,' Florence said, but she caved anyway. 'I did something stupid.'

Lexy waited.

Florence blew out a breath. 'I…um…had a one-night stand.'

'With?'

Florence didn't want to answer that, so she mumbled and looked away.

'And you used protection?'

'Yes. Of course.'

'Not *completely* stupid, then.' Lexy raised an eyebrow. 'Assuming you were both consenting adults, what's the problem?'

Florence groaned. Time to confess all. 'He's

my new colleague. My new *temporary* colleague.'

'And?'

Why didn't her sister get it? Florence covered her face with her hands. 'I just can't believe I did that. Spent the night with someone I hardly know.'

'It probably did you good. It's more than past time you let yourself get over Dan,' Lexy said gently.

'But he's not going to be around for long. This thing—it doesn't have any kind of future.'

'Also not a problem. You could just think of him as your transition man. The fling who helped you move on from Dan,' Lexy said. She frowned. 'Unless you really like him.'

That was the scary thing. Florence rather thought she did. She'd enjoyed talking to him at the departmental Christmas dinner. She'd enjoyed teasing him and flirting. She'd enjoyed kissing him. Making love with him.

And he was the first man she'd actually noticed since Dan.

'I don't know what I think,' she said. Which wasn't a *complete* fib; right then, she was more confused than she ever remembered being.

'Floss, these things happen. Where you work,

it's intense. Like a pressure cooker. Everyone needs to let off steam from time to time.'

'I guess. But I don't do this sort of thing. I don't have flings.'

'Maybe it's time you did.' Lexy look fascinated. 'Have you got any pictures from last night? Is he cute?'

'No pictures—and very cute,' Florence admitted. He was like every movie star or pop star crush she'd had as a teen: tall, dark hair, amazing eyes, amazing cheekbones. A beautiful mouth. And the way he moved…

'He's going to be working at the hospital for a few more weeks, at least. So, if you like each other, you could make it a longer fling instead of a single night,' Lexy suggested.

'I can't do that.' Florence bit her lip. 'And I have to work with him.'

'Plenty of people have relationships with their colleagues, Floss. You're professional enough not to let it get in the way at work.'

'It's not just that. I…um…pretty much bolted this morning. Goodbye and—' She groaned, covering her face with her hands. 'Oh, this is bad. I almost said thank you for…' She choked on the words, embarrassed beyond belief. Her sister was just about the only person in the world she'd admit this to.

'Thank you for the shag?' Lexy burst out

laughing. 'Oh, sweetheart.' She hugged Florence. 'And now you're feeling like a teenager and you don't know what to do about it.'

'Pretty much. I didn't behave well. He offered to order us room service breakfast.'

'That's nice. Thoughtful.'

'And I just bolted.'

'Look on the bright side. It means he'll know you're not used to one-night stands.'

'I feel so stupid.'

'You're human, Floss. We all do things we regret. It's fine.' Lexy smiled at her. 'So tell me about him.'

'There's not much to tell. He's an emergency doctor, he works with me, and apparently he climbs.'

'Why's he temporary?'

'He had a burst appendix when he was out helping in an earthquake zone. It wiped out his kidneys and he needed a transplant. His family's round this way, so he's here for a while to be near them.'

'It sounds as if he's had a rough time.'

Which made Florence feel even worse about running out on him like that. She couldn't even text him to apologise, because now she thought about it she didn't actually have his number.

'What aren't you telling me?' Lexy asked.

Trust her sister to get straight to the point. 'When you have a transplant, you have to take medication to stop your body rejecting the new organ. And it affects your fertility.'

Lexy made the connection immediately. 'So, if you date him and you let yourself fall for him big-time, you're risking another Dan situation.'

At last she got it. 'Yes.'

'Except not everyone reacts like Dan did. This guy might not be a total arse who wouldn't consider IVF or adoption because it threatens his sense of masculinity,' Lexy said. 'You're overthinking this, Floss. If you like the guy, date him. See where it goes.'

'I can't face putting myself in another Dan situation,' Florence said. 'But, on the other hand, I can hardly say to him, hey, we can extend our one-night stand if you like, but first I need to know if you want children—and if you'd be up for IVF with donor sperm, if you didn't freeze your own sperm before the transplant and the immunosuppressants make you infertile.'

'That'd be a teensy bit full-on,' Lexy agreed. 'Does he know about Dan?'

'No. Nobody at the hospital knows what happened in Leeds. Just that I was married before, it didn't work out, and I'm focused on

my work.' And, if she told herself that often enough, Florence was sure she'd be able to do it. Focus on her work and not think about the missing bits of her life.

Lexy hugged her again. 'Honey, I know you're scared. But you can't keep a barrier round yourself for ever. You're the one who's missing out. It's like learning to dance or sewing. You can't do the new step or stitch at first, because it keeps going wrong. But you try again and again. You break it down into little chunks. You practise. And eventually it clicks.'

'Dating isn't anything like learning to dance or sewing,' Florence protested.

'It so is,' Lexy said, and ruffled her hair. 'It's about facing the fear. What's the worst that can happen? You start dating him, you find out that you don't really like each other, and you agree to be just friends.'

No. The worst thing that could happen would be falling in love with him, and finding out that he didn't want children. Which Florence knew was being contrary, because not having a partner in the first place was the quickest way of making sure she didn't have children. 'Uh-huh,' she said.

'Talk to him,' Lexy advised.

'I will,' Florence fibbed.

'Of course it's going to be a bit awkward when you see him next. But smile, ask him if you can go for coffee in your break, and explain you had a bit of a tough time at the end of your marriage and you've forgotten every bit of dating etiquette you ever knew, and can you please start again with a clean slate and maybe go out for a drink one evening after work?'

It sounded so easy when her sister put it like that. So simple. One step after another.

So why did it feel so daunting?

Once Florence had left, Rob had a shower, changed and went to the restaurant for breakfast. He knew he needed to refuel, but he couldn't face the idea of room service on his own. Not after the way Florence had rejected him. He just wanted to get out of that room and away from these uncomfortable feelings.

Coffee and a bacon sandwich restored some of his equilibrium, but not by that much. He packed his overnight bag, tidied the room and went to Reception to settle his bill.

Part of him was tempted to drive to Ashermouth Bay and see Oliver, but he was pretty sure that his twin would have plans with Gemma. He knew they'd both be generous and kind enough to ask him to join them, but

he didn't want to play gooseberry—and he also didn't want to ruin their day with his bad mood.

His parents? No, because his mother would notice he was antsy and she'd fuss.

Friends—apart from the fact that it was several hours' drive to Manchester and there wouldn't be much daylight left when he got there, they'd all be busy either working at the hospital or already out in the peaks.

Climbing.

The thing he missed more than anything. The one thing that could make him feel better. Feeling the wind in his hair, pushing his body to the limits, being at one with the earth. But he also knew he wasn't fit enough to do it, and he wasn't going to be selfish enough to put a rescue team at risk just because he was out of sorts.

Instead, he spent most of Saturday cleaning his flat and hating every minute of it.

The place still didn't feel like home, even after he'd followed through on the ideas of putting family photographs on the mantelpiece. How did his twin manage to make somewhere feel like home within ten minutes, while everything Rob did felt temporary?

'For pity's sake, stop whining and snap out of it,' he told himself crossly. 'You're so, so lucky. You've got a family who loves you as much as you love them—including a brother who loves you enough to give you a kidney so can you function again instead of being stuck in a hospital bed. You're doing the job that gives your life meaning. You've got a roof over your head. You have friends, even if most of them happen to be on the opposite side of the country right now. You have absolutely *nothing* to be miserable about.'

Though the thought wouldn't go.

What was so wrong with him that Florence had backed away from him so fast?

Was it because he'd suggested it being just a one-night thing and she thought it had been a mistake?

And maybe she was right. He didn't have a great track record, How many relationships had he let fizzle out because he hadn't been prepared to put enough effort in? How many women had he hurt—without meaning to—because he hadn't thought about anything but the next challenge, the next adventure?

He still didn't have an answer by the time he saw her again in the department on Monday.

His skin suddenly felt too tight. Awkward didn't even begin to cover it.

'Good morning!' she said, all bright and

breezy and smiley—just as she was with all their other colleagues.

But he noticed that she didn't meet his eyes. Clearly this was awkward for her, too.

No way could he discuss the situation with her, especially here. The last thing he wanted was gossip running like wildfire around the hospital; he might be here only temporarily, but she wasn't, and it wouldn't be fair to make her the centre of gossip.

He was just going to have to make the best of it. Treat her as if she was just any other team member, and not the woman who'd made him feel as if he'd come back properly to life.

He switched into polite professional mode, too. 'Morning.' Hopefully they wouldn't be rostered in Resus together today, where they'd have to work closely together—and, even worse, risk accidentally touching. He was relieved to discover that they were both on Minors, which would mean they were unlikely to see each other unless one of them needed a second opinion, and he could focus on his patients.

All went according to plan until mid-afternoon, when he could hear someone literally bellowing with pain.

'Please excuse me a second,' he said to the patient whose sprained ankle he'd been examining, and headed for the bay where the ambulance had brought in a man whose arm was in a sling but who was clearly in terrific pain because he yelled and swore every time the movement of the trolley affected his arm.

Florence was a few moments in front of him. 'What's happened?' she asked.

'This is Joe, aged forty-five. He's a builder, fell backwards into a hole, and he's hurt his shoulder,' the paramedic said. 'I'm guessing it's a dislocation. We've given some pain relief but it hasn't touched the pain, and we've put his arm in a sling and a blanket between his arm and chest to support it.'

'I've dislocated a shoulder before, playing rugby, and it didn't hurt anything like this,' Joe said, then roared with pain and swore again. 'For pity's sake, please don't move my shoulder! You're killing me!'

'I need to check whether it's a dislocation or a fracture before I can give you any real pain relief,' Florence said. 'So I'm sending you for an X-ray—I'm sorry, you're clearly in a lot of pain, but if you can grit your teeth and put up with it for a few more minutes we'll know what we're dealing with and can treat you properly. If it's a dislocation, we can fix it here—we'll give you a sedative to relax you and pull it back into place. If it's a fracture, you might need surgery. Either way, it's going to take a couple of months to heal because there will be soft tissue damage.'

'OK. Thanks for being honest,' Joe said. 'And I'm sorry for swearing. It just— Argh!'

'Let's get you to X-Ray,' Florence said. 'Is there anyone we can call for you?'

'It's OK. They called my wife from the ambulance and she's on her way in.'

'If it's a dislocation,' Rob said, 'I'll help with the traction.'

She didn't look at him, but nodded. 'Thanks.'

The X-ray files came through on the computer a few minutes later, showing that Joe had indeed dislocated his shoulder—but it was like no dislocation Rob had ever seen before. 'It's wedged,' he said in disbelief. 'No wonder he's in so much pain.'

'I've never seen anything like that in fourteen years of medicine,' she said.

Fourteen years. Assuming that included her years as a student, that made her two years older than him. And, strictly speaking, Florence was his senior, so he'd better listen to her. 'What's the plan?' he asked.

'More pain relief, sedation to relax him, and traction,' she said. This time, she looked at Rob. 'You're sure you're OK to help?'

Oh, for pity's sake. If she hadn't slept with

him, she wouldn't have seen the scar and he wouldn't have told her about the transplant. She'd promised not to treat him any differently—and yet that was exactly what she was doing. Last week, she wouldn't even have questioned whether he was OK to help. He wouldn't be here in the first place if he wasn't OK to work.

So much for thinking that he'd come to a place where they'd see him for himself, not as someone who needed special treatment. Annoyance made him sharp. 'Yes,' he said tightly. 'The information I gave you about my kidney was privileged. I've already told you I would never put a patient at risk, so I'd prefer you not to mention it again. Fortunately nobody else is here to overhear you. I really don't want that information spreading.'

She flinched slightly at the rebuke, and there was a slash of colour across her cheeks. 'I was out of order. Sorry.'

'Apology accepted. We'll draw a line under it and move on,' he said.

And he didn't mean just her comment about his operation. They needed to move on from the weekend. From the mistake they'd both made. The one that loomed between them and made everything awkward and scratchy. He held her gaze for long enough that he hoped she'd worked out what he wasn't saying.

She nodded. 'Agreed.'

'Good.'

She gave Joe a mild sedative and painkiller. 'I think this is going to need three of us.'

Because she still thought he was under par?

Either he'd said it aloud or it was written all over his face, because she said, 'Because it's wedged, and it's going to need more than two people to sort it.'

It was a good call, and he knew he was being oversensitive. 'I'll go and grab someone,' he said.

The first person he found was Ranj, one of the junior doctors. 'Ranj, have you got a minute?' he asked. 'We've got a patient with a dislocated shoulder—it's wedged—and Florence thinks it'll take three of us for the traction.'

'Wedged?' Ranj whistled. 'That sounds horrific.'

'He's in a lot of pain,' Rob said.

'Poor guy. I'll help,' Ranj said, and followed him back to the patient.

Florence was sitting next to Joe, holding his hand and talking him through what they were about to do. 'We'll try to be as fast as we can, Joe, and the sedative should take most of the edge off it,' she said, 'but if you need to swear your head off to get through the traction, do it because none of us will be offended. We've all heard worse. Or tell us the most terrible dad jokes you know. You've got a captive audience and we'll be forced to laugh.'

Rob liked the way she'd assessed Joe's character so quickly and put him at ease; Joe was still clearly in a great deal of pain, but thanks to Florence he was much more relaxed than when he'd first come into the department.

'I can't think of any jokes,' Joe said.

'Right. Then tell us about the best Christmas dinner you've ever had,' she suggested.

'My mum's,' Joe said. 'She does everything you can think of. Loads of veg, all the trimmings, and she does the best roast potatoes in the world. They're fluffy in the middle and crispy on the outside. But don't tell my wife— she's competitive about roast potatoes, and she and Mum fight over the best way to do it.'

'Choose your potato wisely, make sure you have edges when you cut them, shake them after you parboil them and use very hot fat,' she said promptly. 'None of that covering in semolina malarkey.'

So she was a cook? Rob wouldn't have a clue how to do roast potatoes. Not unless you could get them for the microwave.

'I dunno about semolina,' Ranj said, 'but

my mum covers her roast potatoes with a spice mix before she puts them in the oven and they're awesome.'

Between them, they got Joe talking and distracted—and did the traction to unwedge his dislocated shoulder.

'All right. You're done,' Florence said. 'Don't go rolling your shoulder for a few days, but I'd like you to try lifting your arm for me now.'

Joe looked unsure, as if remembering the severe pain last time he'd tried lifting his arm, but he did as she'd asked. 'Oh, my God. I can actually move my arm again and it doesn't hurt!' His grimace turned to a beaming smile. 'That's amazing. Thank you so much.'

'It's still going to hurt a bit when those painkillers and sedative wear off,' Florence warned. 'You're going to need painkillers for a few days. I'm also going to put you in a sling, and you need to rest that arm for the next five days.'

Horror flashed across Joe's face. 'I can't do that! I've got loads to do at work.'

Yeah. Rob knew how that felt: wanting to get on with your job and being told to rest instead. The unbearable frustration. Ranj had gone again, so he felt safe admitting to his past. 'For what it's worth, mate, I've learned the hard way that it's better to do as you're told and rest,' he said quietly. 'Otherwise you end up having to rest even longer to fix the damage you did by doing things too early.'

'You dislocated your shoulder?' Joe asked.

'Burst appendix,' Rob said. 'And there's nothing worse than having to sit about and rest for even longer than you were originally told, and realising it's your own fault for being stubborn and not listening to someone who does actually know better. Trust me.'

'Trust you, you're a doctor?' Joe asked with a grin.

'Something like that.' Rob exchanged a glance with Florence, and felt as if he'd been seared. Her brown eyes were almost sparking with anger. Though it wasn't surprising that she was annoyed. He'd bitten her head off for alluding to his transplant, and here he was shooting his mouth off about precisely the same thing just a few minutes later. What a hypocrite.

'No heavy lifting for at least six weeks,' Florence said. 'It looks as if there's a bit of tissue damage, but hopefully we can manage it with physio—otherwise you'll need surgery.'

'Which means even more time off work?' Joe asked.

'Got it in one,' Florence said. 'I know it's

not what you want to hear, but I'm afraid Dr Langley's right. Healing takes time. I can give you some exercises to do over the next few days to help with stiffness, and I'll refer you to physio.'

'I'll leave you to it and go back to my patient,' Rob said. 'All the best, Joe. And listen to Dr Jacobs. She knows her stuff.' Even if things weren't great between them personally, right now, he respected her professionally.

He went back to his patient with the sprained ankle, strapped it up and gave advice for ongoing care. He tried not to be disappointed that Florence still seemed to be avoiding him. And he lied to Oliver that evening on the phone, saying that he was absolutely fine. He wasn't fine. At all. But he also didn't know how to even start fixing this.

# CHAPTER FOUR

THERE WAS NO thaw between Rob and Florence during the next week.

Maybe he'd been a bit *too* sharp, he thought, snapping at her when she'd asked if he was really OK to help with traction. She clearly hadn't meant it as a dig at him. She'd been concerned about both her patient and her colleague. If he was completely honest with himself, in her shoes he would've asked the same question.

He would've apologised to her, except he was still smarting from the way she'd walked out on him the morning after the Christmas party. Previously, he'd always stayed on friendly terms with anyone he'd dated—well, OK, he hadn't actually *dated* Florence, he'd done it the wrong way round and slept with her before dating her—and it rankled that she'd been so desperate to leave that she hadn't even had breakfast with him the next morning. She'd made it very clear that she didn't want to date him.

Suck it up and move on, he told himself.

He needed to treat her the same as he treated all his other colleagues, or someone would notice and rumours would start flying, which would make things even worse.

He just about managed it.

But on Friday he felt distinctly rough in the middle of his shift. Hot, and shivery, and there was a pain in his lower back.

If a patient with his own medical history had walked into the department with those symptoms, Rob would have sent him straight to the renal department for an urgent consultation.

Was this a sign of the transplant failing? He knew the stats. Twenty per cent of transplants failed in the first year, despite the patient taking medication to stop their body rejecting the new organ.

Intellectually, he knew that it was more likely he'd come down with some other kind of infection; the immunosuppressants he was taking to avoid his body rejecting the transplant meant he was more susceptible to viruses and urinary tract infections. But the fear still rippled through him. What if his body was rejecting Oliver's kidney? Would he end up back on dialysis, stuck in bed and resting for months and months until another kidney was available, resenting every second he was stuck inside?

He didn't want to walk out of his shift, but he wasn't going to be stubborn and leave it too long. He was on an early shift, so he'd finish work mid-afternoon. He'd go and have a chat with the renal team then. In the meantime, he needed to keep going. The best way to get his temperature down a bit and take some of the edge off the pain would be paracetamol. He headed to the staff kitchen, and had just grabbed some water and taken two tablets out of a foil pack when Florence walked in.

'Are you all right?' she asked.

'Fine, thank you.' He winced inwardly as he heard how snippy he sounded. He hadn't meant to be mean.

'You look like crap,' she said.

Right. So she wasn't pulling punches, either.

She gave him a very pointed look. 'So I'll ask you again. Are you all right?'

'I'm not sure,' he admitted. 'I was fine when I came to work.'

'And now?'

He might as well tell her. Then she could tell him that he probably had a bug or a UTI. Confirm his self-diagnosis. And he could go back to work. 'Hot, shivery and there's a bit of a pain in my lower back.'

She took the temperature gun from its box in the first-aid drawer and aimed it at his forehead. 'Thirty-eight point five,' she said, showing him the red screen.

Officially a fever. No wonder he felt hot and shivery.

'Go to the renal department,' she said. 'Now.'

He'd already thought this through. 'I'll go in a couple of hours' time, at the end of my shift.'

'No, you'll go *now*.' She raised her eyebrows. 'I'm in charge of Minors today, and you're on my team, so you'll do as I tell you.'

She was pulling rank on him? For a second, he stared at her in shock. Then he dropped his gaze. 'Bossy,' he muttered.

'It's most likely to be a bug or a UTI, but there's also the chance it's what you fear it is, and you need to get it checked out,' she said. 'I've heard you telling our patients not to be stubborn and do what they're told. So I suggest, *Dr* Langley, that you take your own advice.' She folded her arms. 'Actually—to make sure you do, I'm coming with you.'

'You don't need to do that.'

'Yes, I do. I'm responsible for my team's well-being.'

He shook his head. 'I'm in the middle of my shift. I can't just walk out and leave everyone to pick up the slack.'

'You're on an early.' She glanced at her watch. 'That means we've got three hours until you were done anyway. If they sign you off, we can manage until the end of the shift. And I haven't had my break yet, so I'm taking it now. We're going to the renal department.'

He was feeling rough enough to give in gracefully and let her usher him to the renal department.

'Let me know when he's done,' she said to the secretary, 'and I'll sort out transport.'

'I can dr—' he began, then stopped as she gave him a very pointed look. Since when could brown eyes freeze you like that?

Florence Jacobs could be seriously scary.

Though she was absolutely right. Of course he couldn't drive. He was way too distracted with pain and worry, and he'd be a danger to other road users.

'Thank you,' he said instead.

'You're welcome. I'd better get back to the department.'

And she still hadn't had a rest from work. She'd spent her break looking after him. 'I'm sorry,' he said.

'There's nothing to apologise for. When

you're feeling rough at work, you need a colleague to look out for you,' she said.

Which put him in his place. She'd just made it clear that she saw him as a colleague, and a temporary one at that.

Though he knew she could've just left him to struggle on. Instead, she'd helped him. Bossily, but she'd helped him.

'I'll see you later,' she said, and left him to the ministrations of the renal department.

Rob Langley must feel absolutely dreadful if he was actually listening to her and doing what she suggested, Florence thought.

What she'd said to him was true enough. She would've done the same for any of her colleagues who were feeling ill on shift: made sure they were OK, and arranged cover if there were more than a couple of hours of their shift left.

But she still felt guilty about the way she'd behaved towards Rob almost a fortnight ago. She'd bolted from his hotel room, the morning after they'd spent the night together, without any explanation. He'd done nothing wrong, and she'd treated him badly. And she'd been starchy with him ever since, thanks to a mixture of awkwardness and shame. He'd snapped at her for nearly breaking his confidence, and that had stung enough for her to avoid him as much as possible.

Perhaps now was their chance to get back on an even keel.

She took the head of their department to one side to let him know that Rob was in the renal department, getting checked over, then got on with her shift.

The renal team called literally two minutes after the end of her shift. Perfect timing. She did the handover, then headed to the renal department to find Rob. He was sitting in the waiting area, looking terrible.

Did that mean he'd had bad news? Was his body rejecting his brother's kidney?

'How are you doing?' she asked.

'Fairly rubbish,' he admitted. 'They've run all the tests. The good news is that it's just an infection and they can give me something to clear it up.'

Not that his transplant was failing. He must be so relieved. 'Glad to hear it.'

'But the bad news,' he said with a grimace, 'is that they're signing me off for a week to recuperate.'

'Which is probably sensible,' she said.

'Rest is a four-letter word. Literally and metaphorically,' he said. 'Remember the guy with the dislocated shoulder who hated the idea of being off work for a few days? I know exactly how he felt.'

'You don't have any choice. Suck it up, Dr Langley,' she said.

Which told him.

'And I'll give you a lift,' she added. 'Lucky for you I'm on an early as well, and I've done my handover, so you don't have to go and wait for me in the cafeteria or anything until my shift is done.'

'Thank you,' he said. 'I owe you.'

She shook her head. 'It's what any colleague would do for another. You'd do the same for me. Where do you want me to take you? You said your parents live near here. Shall I drop you there?'

He rubbed a hand across his face. 'Don't take this the wrong way. I love my mum and dad dearly. I'd do anything for them. But my mum practically cocooned me after the transplant and I couldn't stand it. It's why I found myself a short-term flat lease when I started the job here. I really can't face going home to my parents. Mum'll go into panic mode and drive me crazy, and the last thing I want to do is snap at her and hurt her when I know she loves me and she's got my best interests at heart.'

She liked the fact he clearly knew himself

well, and was thinking of his mother's feelings. 'Your brother's, then?'

'He's busy at work. Anyway, he's already done more than enough, giving me a kidney.' He lifted one shoulder in a casual shrug. 'I admit that I appreciate the lift, but I'll be fine on my own in my flat.'

She disagreed. 'Rob, you're feeling rough now and you're brewing an infection, so you've probably got a couple of days of feeling even worse before the meds kick in. If you feel anywhere near as terrible as you look, you need someone else around.' But Rob was stubborn. Telling him would put his back up, or make him do the equivalent of sticking his fingers in his ears and singing 'La, la, I can't hear you'. She'd appeal to the clinician in him, so it would be his own idea. 'If you had a patient in this position, what would you recommend? Would you be happy for your patient to be on their own?'

'No.'

Before she realised it, the words were out. 'Then that leaves us with just one solution. Come and stay with me.'

Had his consultant just given him something that had a side-effect of hallucinations? Rob wondered. Had Florence Jacobs just invited him to stay with her?

But they weren't even friends. They were temporary colleagues. And they'd had a one-night stand almost a fortnight ago that had made her back away from him so fast, there had practically been scorch marks under her feet. Why on earth would she invite him to stay with her?

'I'm sorry. Did you just…?'

Colour flooded through her face. 'I haven't been very fair to you. Very nice to you. So it's…' She blew out a breath. 'Look, there aren't any strings. It's what I'd do for any other colleague in your situation.'

Including one she'd slept with?

But she'd just specifically said no strings.

Maybe it was because he was feeling rough that his head wasn't working properly and he couldn't quite understand what she meant.

He'd probably said it out loud, because she clarified, 'It means if you feel really rough, you won't be on your own—you'll be staying with someone who's a medic and will know when to panic and when to back off.'

Which was a good point, he knew. It was why he ought to ring his brother. But he didn't want to risk getting in the way of Oliver's happiness, the way he had before—even though

Gemma was very different from Tabby, Rob still didn't want to put a burden on Oliver.

And staying with Florence meant he'd get the chance to know her better.

He knew it wasn't sensible—but it was too much of a temptation to resist.

'No cotton wool?' he checked.

'I'm not a fan of the stuff outside work,' she said. 'It's not eco-friendly. The bleaching and mixing means it doesn't biodegrade. Bamboo cloths or muslin are better.'

He couldn't help smiling. 'Good point. OK. Thank you. That'd be nice. As long as you let me contribute. I'm not a great cook, but I can do the basics. I'll do my share.'

'Apart from the fact you're not well enough, you're my guest,' she said.

'Guests always bring something nice for their host.' He shrugged. 'Perhaps I can pay for some takeaways to be delivered, then.'

'We'll argue about that later. Let's go while you can still stand up.'

He liked the fact that she was brisk with him.

He liked *her*.

But he still wanted to know why she'd been so desperate to escape that Saturday morning.

Maybe spending time at her place and get-ting to know each other meant she'd feel comfortable telling him whatever had spooked her—and then they could move on. Maybe take things forward. Because the more time he spent with her, the more he realised he liked her. And Florence was the first woman in years who'd intrigued him enough to want more from a relationship.

'Would it be OK to stop at my flat and pick up some clean clothes and my medication?' he asked.

'Yes, of course.'

They didn't chat on the way to his place, once he'd given her the postcode for her sat-nav, but it was a comfortable silence rather than an awkward one. And he noted that Florence was as competent and confident when driving as she was in an emergency room, saving a life.

At his flat, she refused his offer of a mug of coffee. He packed an overnight bag quickly with a couple of changes of clothing, his medication, his laptop and a couple of books.

'You pack light, I see,' she said with a smile.

He shrugged. 'I learned that from climbing; keep it light and keep it simple, so you have room for the important stuff.'

'That's a good life lesson,' she said.

What did that mean? She'd said that night that she had unwanted baggage...

He shot her a sidelong glance, but her expression was unreadable. And now wasn't the time to probe—not when he was feeling like death warmed up and he was likely to misread all the signals. Better to keep his mouth shut.

By the time she parked the car, all he wanted to do was to curl up in a ball and sleep for a month.

'You look all in,' Florence said gently. 'Come and sit down. I'll get you a hot drink and something to eat.'

'Thank you, but I'm not really hungry,' he said.

'You need to eat, and so do I, so you might as well eat with me,' she said firmly. 'Is there anything you don't eat?'

'Grapefruit,' he said, 'because of the medication I'm on, and for the same reasons I'm keeping my salt intake low. Other than that I eat anything.' As far as he was concerned, apart from good chocolate and cake, food was merely fuel. There was a world out there to conquer, and Rob wasn't going to waste time selecting herbs, chopping them finely, and decorating the top of every dish. Any more than five minutes in a microwave or a stir-fry pan, and the recipe wasn't for him.

'Let's go.' She took his bag and ushered him inside, and he didn't have the energy to protest that he could carry his own bag—especially because he knew that right at that moment it would sap his already diminishing energy.

'The guest room is here on the left,' she said, setting his bag down and indicating the door. 'Mine's next to it, the bathroom's opposite, and the kitchen and living room are at the end of the hallway. Take your time to freshen up, then come and sit down when you're ready. I'll be in the kitchen.'

'Thanks.' He opened the door and smiled. He had a feeling her guest room was geared to her nieces, as the double bed had a bright pink duvet and there were three teddies wearing leotards, tutus and ballet shoes sitting on the pillows; each teddy had an initial embroidered on the leotard. He had a sudden vision of three little girls all cuddled up in that big wide bed with their teddies, and Florence sitting on the end of the bed, reading them a story.

And then his head morphed that into something even weirder. Three little girls with his own blue eyes...

No, no and absolutely no.

Clearly the infection had addled his brain as well as threatening his kidney. Since when did he ever fantasise about settling down and having kids? He spent his time working and climbing. There wasn't time for a family in the middle. He'd never met anyone who'd tempted him to want to settle down and have kids. And, if he ever did, he'd expected it to be someone who was a fellow adventure junkie, not someone who was domesticated and settled.

Yet the woman in his fantasies had been Florence.

Slightly spooked, he concentrated on hanging up his clothes and putting his wash bag in Florence's bathroom, then splashed his face with water. He still felt terrible, but he could hardly just crawl under the covers and sink into oblivion. The very least he should do was tell Florence that he was heading for bed. He went to the kitchen, and discovered her busy doing something on the stove.

'Something smells nice,' he said.

'It's a quick dish: pasta with lemon and asparagus. I'm adding some sautéed chicken to give it a bit more protein, so it'll still be light on your digestion but nutritious,' she said. 'Three more minutes and it'll be done.'

From his mum, this would've felt like fussing and made him feel smothered; from Florence, it felt thoughtful and made him feel cosseted. It was a weird sensation, and he wasn't sure whether it worried him or settled him. His head was all over the place. That momentary vision of three little girls—their daughters—was definite proof that he was ill.

'Is there anything I can do to help?' he asked.

'Just sit down at the table,' she said. 'This pretty much looks after itself. Do you want tea or coffee?'

'I...' He blew out a breath. 'Sorry, right now I'm too tired even to think, let alone make a decision.'

'Water, then,' she said, and added a slice of lemon to the glass.

He went over to the table—which she'd already laid—and sat down, grateful.

She'd given him space, with no pressure.

If there hadn't been the awkwardness between them, he would've hugged her. But he didn't want to risk making it even more awkward. 'Thank you,' he said. 'I appreciate this so much.'

'You're welcome.'

'I like the bears with tutus.'

She winced. 'Sorry. I'll move them and change the duvet cover to something more masculine.'

He laughed, then winced as it hurt. 'It's not going to kill me to sleep under a pink duvet cover. I take it your nieces sometimes come and stay?'

'Yes.' She gestured to the fridge. 'And they're the ones who've drawn me those lovely pictures.'

He glanced over and did a double-take. 'Is that a dinosaur in a tutu?'

'Oh, yes. That's one you might not have come across before—a ballet-saurus.' She grinned. 'Margot loves dinosaurs even more than she loves ballet. Lexy and I took the girls to see the animatronic dinosaurs at the Natural History Museum in London over the summer, and Margot was in seventh heaven.'

He could imagine it. Florence, making a fuss of her nieces, taking them on days out and reading them stories. Domestic. The kind of things that usually made him want to run a mile because he liked to be in the big wide world, untrammelled, pushing himself to the limit.

But his life was going to have to change. And he was going to have to come to terms with being boxed in, at least for the next week.

'Margot's the oldest, isn't she?' he said. 'Then Anna and Darcey.'

She looked pleased that he'd remembered. 'That's right.'

And then he found himself wondering: if Florence had a daughter, would she name her after a ballerina?

Oh, for pity's sake. It was none of his business. And he didn't want to think about Florence having babies. Particularly as he was still spooked by that vision of his own three small daughters...

The pasta was amazing. Rob didn't usually pay much attention to food, other than good chocolate, but this was something else. 'This is fabulous,' he said.

'It's a very easy recipe.' Florence looked at him. 'You're not a cook, then?'

'I'm too busy to spend time in the kitchen. Ollie's the cook, not me, and he loves his gadgets. I'm very good at sticking TV dinners in the microwave, though,' he said. 'Or I can do stir-fry. Anything that takes less than five minutes.'

'Got you.' She looked at him. 'So is that because you'd rather spend your time climbing than skivvying in the kitchen?'

'Yes. Though climbing is still off the cards for a while.' He grimaced. 'I'd never be stupid enough to climb on my own and put the rescue team at risk, but I also know I'm not fit enough to manage the kind of routes I enjoy most—so I'd slow any climbing partners down to the point where none of us would enjoy it. And I'm sensible enough to know that if I push myself too hard, too fast, I'm going to end up in an even worse state than I am right now and have to wait even longer before I get my life back. But...' He grimaced again. 'It's still frustrating.'

'You miss it?'

'More than anything. Climbing, for me, is like breathing,' he said.

'I've never climbed,' she said. 'The most I've ever done is walk up and down the steep cliff paths at Ashermouth Bay.'

Which was nothing like climbing: cliff paths were simply a difficult walk without any of the fun. How could he explain it to her? 'It's the most amazing feeling. Pushing your body to its limits, getting to the top of a climb, and knowing you've earned that spectacular view,' he said.

'So kind of like a runner's high?'

'Better than that. The only thing like it is sex.'

Oh, no.

How could he have just said that?

'I—um—' He didn't dare look at her.

'A climb is as good as a climax?'

She sounded amused, so he risked a look. 'Yes.' And then he wished he'd kept his mouth shut when she met his gaze. Because it looked as if she was remembering that night. And he could remember every second of pleasure they given each other. It shocked him to realise just how much he wanted to experience it all again.

Did *she*?

Was that faint hint of colour in her cheeks telling him that she, too, had been thrown by what had happened between them?

But he couldn't ask. Not now, when he was barely capable of standing up, let along carrying her to her bed. He needed this conversation to be back to a neutral subject. Fast. Before he said something that caused an unholy mess. 'Can I do the washing-up?'

'No. Not just because you're a guest, but because you look absolutely exhausted. Go and sit on the sofa,' she directed. 'Feel free to put whatever you want on the TV.'

'I would normally argue,' he said, 'but I admit this bug has knocked me for six.' And he hated it. He hated feeling so weak. The words burst out of him. 'It feels like it did when my kidneys first packed up. I can't bear to think of having to rest for ages again. This just isn't me. I'm really not this weak, *pathetic* individual.'

'Go and sit down. It's fine,' she said gently. 'And, just for the record, resting doesn't make you weak or pathetic. It means you're being sensible and giving your body a chance to heal.'

'I guess,' he lied. He still hated feeling weak and vulnerable and having to rely on other people. He was strong and capable; he was the fixer, not the fixee.

'Rob, do you think your patients are weak and pathetic?' she asked.

He frowned. 'No. Of *course* not. They're ill or they've been in an accident and they need my help.'

'And the difference between them and your situation is…?'

He didn't have an answer for that, so he huffed out a breath.

'Don't be so hard on yourself,' she said gently. 'Go and sit down.'

'OK,' he muttered, and went into the living room. It was comfortable and cosy; the mantelpiece was crammed with framed photographs that he guessed were of her family and the people closest to her, but he didn't have the energy to be nosey and have a proper look.

*Resting doesn't make you weak. It means you're being sensible and giving your body a chance to heal.*

She'd been kind. She'd tried to settle some of his restlessness.

And she was right. He wouldn't judge his patients in the same way that he judged himself.

He needed to apologise to her for being snippy and difficult. And he intended to fill her house with flowers to make up for being a rubbish house guest.

He switched on the TV and flicked through the channels until he found a nature documentary, then settled back on the sofa to wait for her to join him. Although he tried to keep his eyelids open, they seemed to have a mind of their own and kept closing. He blinked hard, but they simply refused to stay open…

Florence finished washing up, drying the crockery and cutlery and putting it away.

From the sounds in the room next door, Rob was watching the kind of documentary she liked, too. Finding something in common with her temporary house guest would be a good idea.

But, when she went to join him, she discovered he was sound asleep on the sofa.

She tucked a throw round him; he murmured in his sleep, but he didn't wake.

He looked absolutely exhausted. She'd let him rest for a while, then wake him so he could go to bed, she decided. She curled up in the chair and watched the documentary, though she couldn't concentrate on it properly; she was way too aware of the man sleeping on her sofa.

A man who hated resting and said that he was happiest when he was busy.

A man who had craved adventure, given that he'd worked for a humanitarian aid organisation and loved climbing.

The man she'd made love with, two short weeks ago. The man who'd be sleeping in the room opposite hers, only few steps away…

No. She wasn't going to let herself think about bed and Robert Langley in the same sentence. She'd invited him to stay purely because he was ill, he was her colleague and he needed a bit of support. She wasn't attracted to him. Her heart didn't skitter every time she looked at him. The way his mouth had felt against her was totally irrelevant.

And if she told herself that often enough, she'd start to believe it.

Perhaps.

An hour later, she shook his shoulder gently until he woke.

'Wh…?' He blinked at her, his eyes fuzzy with sleep.

'Go to bed,' she said gently. 'Or you'll get

a crick in your neck that'll annoy you all day tomorrow.'

'I…' He blinked again, as if trying to focus. 'Sorry. I didn't mean to crash out on you.'

'No need to apologise. I let you sleep for a bit because you looked too exhausted to move, but I wouldn't leave you on the sofa all night.'

He stared at the throw she'd placed round him. 'You put a blanket over me.'

'So you didn't get cold. I don't want my house guest complaining about the lack of services,' she quipped, trying to keep it light.

He followed her lead. 'Don't worry. I'll leave you a review on all the hospitality websites saying that you're a hostess who goes above and beyond.'

His smile was the sweetest, loveliest thing she'd ever seen. So much for keeping this light and teasing. If she wasn't careful, she'd fall for him. Which would be a very bad move.

'I'll see you tomorrow. And thank you, Florence. For looking after me without making me feel miserable and mollycoddled. I can't begin to tell you how much I appreciate that.' This time, there was an intensity in his gaze that made her stomach swoop.

'No problem,' she said. And she really hoped he didn't hear the slight squeak in her voice. 'See you tomorrow. I'll let you have the bathroom first. Feel free to use anything you like, and the towels are all clean.'

'Cheers.' He still looked terrible, but not quite as bone-deep tired as he had earlier. 'See you tomorrow.'

# CHAPTER FIVE

ROB WOKE THE next MORNING, his head all woozy. He was still hot and shivery, but he felt slightly better than he had the day before. Until he glanced at his watch and realised that it was half-past ten. Apart from the fact that he never slept this late, he was Florence's guest. Lying in bed all day and keeping her waiting around to dance attendance on him was incredibly selfish.

Really, he ought to get up and go home.

He dragged himself out of bed and into the bathroom, showered and cleaned his teeth, then dressed swiftly and went to find Florence. She was sitting in a chair by the window in the living room, holding a wooden hoop in her left hand and concentrating on something; he watched her for a moment and realised that she was stitching. Rob had never met anyone who sewed before.

'Morning,' she said, smiling at him.

That smile did weird things to his insides. Weird things he wasn't comfortable thinking about. He didn't react to people like this. 'Morning,' he muttered. 'Sorry I slept in.'

'It's fine. You're ill. It probably did you a lot of good, getting some rest. How are you feeling?'

'A lot better,' he said.

She raised an eyebrow. 'Want to let your common sense answer, rather than your pride?'

In other words, he still looked as bad as he felt. Busted. 'Better than yesterday,' he said, 'but, OK, I admit it: not that much.'

'These things take time,' she said.

Yes. And resting made him feel so boxed in and miserable. He hated being still. Always had, always would. Oh, to be halfway up a mountain somewhere…

'What would you like for breakfast?' she asked.

'I don't expect you to wait on me,' he said. 'It's more than enough that you offered to let me stay with you for a few days. I'll sort myself out.' Then he thought about it. She was at home at this time on a Saturday. She hadn't said anything yesterday about being on a late shift today. 'Are you off duty today?'

'Yes.'

Oh, no. 'So does that mean you've had to cancel your plans because of me?'

'They were movable,' she said.

So she *had* had to cancel her plans. He groaned. 'I'm so sorry. I didn't mean to ruin your day off.'

'You haven't ruined it. I'd tell you if there was a problem.'

He wasn't so sure. She hadn't told him what the problem was when she'd bolted, the weekend before last; and the subject had remained off limits between them ever since. But he felt too rough right now to deal with emotional stuff, so he decided to take what she'd said at face value. 'OK. Thanks.'

'Help yourself to whatever you want in the kitchen.'

'Thanks. Can I make you a coffee?'

'That would be lovely,' she said. 'A splash of milk, no sugar, please.'

'Toast?'

'Apart from the fact I've had breakfast,' she said, nodding at her sewing, 'I need to keep my hands clean for this.'

'What are you making?'

'A ballet-saurus for Margo.' She lifted the hoop to show him a blob of stitches in various shades of green and pink.

Was that meant to be a dinosaur wearing a

tutu, like the drawing he'd seen on her fridge last night? 'I'm glad you told me what it was,' he said, 'because I'm afraid I wouldn't have guessed.'

Florence chuckled, and Rob realised just how pretty she was. She sparkled, and that smile made the whole room feel as if it had just lit up. It made him want to walk over to her and kiss her—which was the last thing he should do. The last time they'd kissed, it had all been wonderful—and then it all gone badly wrong. Staying here would give him a chance to find out what the problem was, and he couldn't afford to blow it by giving in to his impulses. He made them both a mug of coffee and took hers in to her.

'Thanks. That's perfect,' she said, giving him another of the smiles that made him feel all quivery.

He tried not to think about that and watched her sew. Though that too was a mistake, because her fingers were so clever, so deft—and it made him think about how those fingers had felt against his skin. How she'd touched him, heated his blood. How much he wanted to repeat that.

She glanced up and noticed him watching her. 'What?'

He definitely wasn't going to tell her what

was in his head. 'I've never seen anyone sit and sew before,' he said instead.

'Not your mum or any of your girlfriends?'

He shook his head. 'One of my exes used to knit things, but she got very offended when I didn't wear a sweater she'd made for me to climb in. I explained that wicking material was much more efficient at regulating my temperature and a lot lighter than the sweater she'd knitted, and I didn't mean to offend her...but she was still hugely upset with me. She dumped me, two days later.'

'I can see both points of view—she'd tried to do something nice for you and of course she'd be upset that you didn't like it, but maybe she should've checked with you before doing all that work.' Florence raised an eyebrow. 'Remind me never to cross-stitch anything for you.'

'You mean, make me a blob I won't appreciate?'

She laughed and indicated her sewing. 'I know this looks like a blob. It's the back stitching—the little bits of detail—that'll bring it to life. When it's done, Margot will love it.' She put the hoop down, picked up her phone and scrolled through it. 'Here. I did this one for my best friend's birthday. This is before and after adding the detail.'

He looked at the blocks of colour, then at the peacock with all the iridescent colours and the delicate fronds on its tail feathers. 'That's impressive. It must've taken you a long time.'

'It got me through my divorce, last year.' And then she looked shocked, as if she hadn't meant to say that.

Was that what she'd meant about baggage?

He needed to tread carefully: acknowledge what she'd said, but not say anything that could be considered in the slightest bit judgemental. Give her an opening, if she wanted to talk—and he would most definitely listen, but not make her feel under any obligation. 'Uh-huh.'

When she didn't elaborate—and it was none of his business anyway, he reminded himself—he said, 'So have you done sewing like that for very long?'

'Years,' she said. 'Mum taught Lexy and me when we were teenagers, as a stress-reliever. It got us through our exams. It's like counting dance steps, or counting reps in the gym. You have to concentrate on counting the stitches and there isn't any room left in your head for your worries. It gives you a proper mental break.'

'That's what climbing's like, too,' Rob said. 'I concentrate on where I'm going to put my hands and my feet; I guess it's like you have to concentrate on where you put your needle.'

She gave him a wry smile. 'Except if I go wrong I can just unpick a few stitches, whereas if you go wrong there's going to be pain and possibly broken bones.'

'Not if you belay properly—fixing your rope, so if you slip you won't fall far,' he added in explanation, seeing the confusion flit across her expression when he mentioned belaying. 'But, yes, it's the same thing. You have to concentrate on what you're doing.'

'And at the end of it you've got something to show for it, and you don't feel guilty about wasting your time, the way you might feel guilty if you'd just spent a couple of hours playing games on your phone,' she said.

That was exactly how he felt about climbing. 'It's the buzz of achieving something,' he said. 'Pushing yourself further—though does that happen in sewing?'

'It can. You start by making something simple in one or two colours, and you work up to stitching something more complex with maybe lots of very similar colours,' she said. 'Or create your own patterns rather than just following someone else's. It's the same feeling.' She paused. 'Since you're here for a few days, I could teach you how to sew.'

'I can't stay here for a few days,' Rob said, aghast. 'That's way too big an imposition.'

'OK,' she said. 'If you want to be stubborn about it—not to mention stupid—you can always call a taxi and leave this morning. And then, when you've collapsed and someone has to ring your brother from the hospital to tell him where you are, you can explain to him that not only were you ill in the first place and didn't tell him, you also refused a colleague's help. My guess is he'll go for the big guns and call your mum.' She shrugged. 'Maybe that's what you actually want in the first place, despite all your protests.'

He shuddered. 'No. *Really* no.' He looked at her. 'Sorry. I don't mean to sound ungrateful. I feel guilty about being a burden on you. You had to change your plans today because of me.'

'You're not a burden. If I was the one who was ill and could do with someone just to be there for a few days in case I needed help, you'd offer to do it, wouldn't you?'

How could she be so sure that he was that nice? Though he thought about it. Of course he'd offer to help. He was a bit single-minded, but he was a team player too and he wasn't completely selfish. 'I guess.'

She looked at him. 'You're not well enough

right now even to walk to the park, but I think you need something physical to do, to distract you. That's why I suggested teaching you to sew.'

Sewing. He couldn't quite get his head round the idea. 'Forgive me for being rude, Florence, but men don't sew.'

'I'll remember that next time you're suturing someone's forehead,' she said dryly.

He laughed. 'I don't mean *that* kind of stitching. That's more like tying knots and doing it neatly so your patient has minimal scarring. I can do that, no problem.'

'OK—but you're still wrong,' she said. 'There was the guy in the POW camp in the Second World War who made samplers and he stitched rude messages about Hitler in Morse code in the borders.'

'Seriously?'

'Seriously. And it was my grandfather who taught my mum how to sew. His doctor was way ahead of her time and recommended it to help him relax. So don't genderise sewing.'

'Got it.'

'And right now you're stuck resting. You're bored.'

That didn't even begin to describe how he felt. Fidgety. Unable to settle. Filled with fear that it was all going wrong and he'd end up back on dialysis again, and he'd be stuck waiting for months for another replacement kidney and feeling the walls close more and more tightly round him when he was desperate to be outside in the mountains. And underneath it all something else that he wasn't used to dealing with: his growing feelings towards Florence. That made him twitchy, too.

'Why not give this a try?'

He thought about the needlework he'd seen on the walls in stately homes while accompanying his parents. 'But isn't it all alphabets and flowers?'

'Grandad liked stitching birds and dogs. But, if you're going to be stereotypical about it, you can stitch a motorbike, or a car, or...' She gave him a pointed look. 'A tiger.'

That was how he felt. Like a caged tiger. Had she realised that? If so, she was maybe the first person ever to see what made him tick. And he wasn't sure whether that excited him or unnerved him more.

'Start with something simple to get the hang of the technique. A bookmark would give you a quick result, so you get the hit of finishing.'

'Are you saying I'm impatient?'

She lifted an eyebrow. 'Aren't you?'

Not at work; but, in his private life, he supposed he was. Though he'd never understood why. 'OK. If you've got the time, then thank you. It'd be lovely if you taught me.'

'You're on.' Leaving her stitching on the table by her side, she went to the sideboard and took out some material, a box filled with threads, and a file. 'What do you want to stitch?'

'I'll be guided by you,' he said.

She opened the file and took out a pattern. Her huge brown eyes glittered with mischief as she met his gaze. 'Something simple, then. A stylised rose.' She opened the box of threads so he could see the colours better. 'Pick two colours.'

He noticed now how much pink there was in her living room. Cushions. The rug. The curtains.

And he knew she was expecting him to choose a traditionally masculine colour.

Given her comment about not genderising things, he wondered if her ex had done that. He'd heed her warning and not make the same mistake.

'Pink or red for a rose, right?' he asked.

'There's no reason why you can't stitch a blue rose if you want to. Or yellow. Or orange. And the leaves don't have to be green, either.'

'Hey. You told me not to genderise.' He smiled. 'Anyway, my mum's favourite flow-

ers are pink roses. Maybe I can make something for her.'

'A motif like this—if you repeat it three
times, it'd make a nice bookmark,' she said.
'I can give you a demo first, if you like, or
you can just go straight in and I'll talk you
through.'

Talking it through. He had a feeling they
weren't just talking about sewing. Well, they
were on the surface—but Rob knew it went
deeper than that. And, if this was the key to
understanding her more, he was all for it.
'Straight in,' he said.

She talked him through setting up the strip
of material in a hoop and where to start working on the pattern. Putting a needle through
holes that were already there in the material
sounded simple. It *was* simple. And he picked
it up quickly enough that Florence didn't need
to talk him through more than two rows.

He started to find a rhythm: and then it
ground to a halt. The stitching didn't look how
hers did, all neat and flat and shiny. And he
didn't understand where he'd gone wrong. The
more he looked at it, the less he could work
it out.

She glanced over at him. 'Problem?'

'Yes. But I don't know what,' he admitted.

'Let's have a look.' She peered at it. 'OK.

You've done a couple of stitches the wrong way round, which is why it looks a bit uneven, and you haven't been entirely accurate with your needle placement—my guess is you're trying to stitch as fast as you can. It's not a race, Rob. It's about finding a rhythm and filling your head. Unpick this back to where you went wrong, and try again.'

He did.

And he had to unpick things several times.

But then he started to get what she meant. There was a rhythm to this, like climbing. He had to concentrate on what he was doing, so there wasn't enough room in his head for the frustration and impatience that had been overwhelming him. And he could see the simple shape of a stylised rose taking shape on the fabric as he worked, all pink and perfect.

Part of him would've loved to send a selfie of him sewing to his twin. But then he would have to admit both to the infection and to the fact that he was staying with Florence; and he wasn't ready to pick his way through all the complicated explanations that would entail. So he concentrated on the sewing. Stitch by stitch by stitch.

This was surreal, Florence thought. If anyone had told her a month ago that she'd be giving needlework lessons to a man like Robert Langley—and in her own living room, to boot—she would've laughed.

But here they were.

She could tell how frustrated he was by the constraints of his health, and this was the second-best distraction she could think of. Her first choice of distraction was completely inappropriate; though it hadn't helped when Rob had compared the rush of climbing to the feel of an orgasm. She could remember exactly what it had felt like when Rob had touched her or brushed his mouth against her skin, and the memories made her ache.

Right now, she was so aware of Rob. The warmth of his body. The scent of his skin. His height. Those stunning blue eyes.

And when she'd touched his hand earlier to guide him with the needle, it had felt as if she'd been galvanised.

Had he felt it, too? That tingle starting on the skin and running the whole length of each nerve? Did he want to touch her as much as she wanted to touch him?

Oh, for pity's sake. The man was *ill*. The last thing he needed was for her to hit on him. She ought to treat him as a patient. Even if her body was urging her to treat him like a lover. Not to mention that he was the last person she should let herself fall for. If she was going to risk her heart again, it would be with someone who wanted the same things that she did: to settle down and have a family.

She supposed that was academic, because she didn't actually want to trust someone with her heart again. She'd felt so worthless and unlovable after Dan's betrayal; not only hadn't she been enough for him, he hadn't wanted to have children with her. She hadn't been able to work out just what was so wrong with her that he hadn't wanted her, and she'd closed in on herself over the last couple of years. To trust someone with herself again was akin to climbing a mountain. She didn't want to take that risk.

Though she still wanted Rob.

It wasn't possible. She couldn't have Rob without the risk. And there was no guarantee he wanted a relationship with her. He was here on a temporary contract; but she was pretty sure that he'd go back to his old life in Manchester rather than renewing his contract or looking for a permanent job here. He'd move on. And she'd be left behind.

Better to suppress the longings.

'So is it helping?' she asked, when she'd had to unpick a row for the third time because she couldn't concentrate with him next to her.

'Surprisingly, yes,' he said. 'If anyone had told me that sewing would be fun, I wouldn't have believed them.' He shook his head. 'If Ollie could see me now...'

Even though he didn't finish the sentence, she could guess what he meant. 'Your brother wouldn't laugh at you,' she said.

'No. He's one of the good guys. And much nicer than I am,' Rob said.

'You're hardly a bad guy, Rob,' she said.

'No? I'm the reason my brother's wedding got cancelled.'

She stared at him, surprised. 'Why?' She was pretty sure it wasn't because Rob had had a fling with the bride-to-be. Apart from the fact he was clearly close to his brother, he wasn't the sort to lie and cheat. What you saw was what you got.

He sighed. 'Because Ollie gave me a kidney. And Tabby—his fiancée—panicked that he'd become ill and she'd have to look after him.'

Florence frowned. 'That's a bit shallow, as well as very misinformed. The donee rather than the donor is the one who's more likely to have problems after a transplant.'

'Ollie says he can understand why she panicked. Her dad has chronic fatigue syndrome and her mum has had to give him an awful lot of support over the years. Tabby didn't want that sort of life for herself. But I agree with you. I think Tabby was shallow and a bit on the selfish side, and she definitely wasn't right for my brother.' He sighed. 'I just hate that Ollie got hurt when she called everything off. And that wouldn't have happened if I hadn't needed a kidney.'

Guilt mingled with pain glittered in his eyes. But it wasn't Rob's fault that his brother's fiancée had got cold feet. 'Maybe,' Florence said carefully, 'your brother had a lucky escape. Because surely it would've been worse if they'd got married and he'd thought everything was fine, and then life threw a curveball and she walked away?'

'I guess,' Rob said. 'Thankfully he's met someone else now. Someone who loves him for who he is. Who understands him. Who cherishes him.'

Was it her imagination, or did Rob sound wistful? And, if she was right, was that wistfulness because he wanted someone to feel that way about him, too? Was that why he'd never settled down before—because nobody had made him feel like that?

Not that it was any of her business.

'It's good to have someone who always has your back,' she said. 'Someone who won't let you down.'

* * *

That sounded heartfelt.

And Florence had said this morning that she was divorced.

Had her husband let her down? There wasn't a nice way of asking, and the last thing Rob wanted to do was to make her feel awkward or bring back any bad memories.

Then, to his surprise, she said, 'I owe you an apology.'

He frowned. 'For what?'

'For…' She squirmed slightly, and her cheeks went very pink. 'That Saturday morning. I… um…bolted.'

'Yes, you did,' he said, trying to make his voice sound as neutral as possible.

'It wasn't a nice thing to do. And I'm sorry.'

'You don't need to apologise—' though he was really gratified that she had '—and I'm sure you had your reasons.'

'I…' She dragged in a breath. 'Baggage, I guess. You're the first person I've slept with since I split up with Dan.'

Dan, he presumed, was her ex-husband. And Rob was the first man she'd slept with since the split?

That changed things.

Significantly.

Florence clearly wasn't the sort of person

who followed her impulses, the way he did. Spending the night with him had been out of character for her. What had made her do it? Had the attraction between them been strong enough to overcome her common sense? Did she regret it? Well, of course she'd regretted it, because she'd bolted the morning after. But she'd had time to think about it now. So what did she want? A fling to help her get past whatever had gone wrong with her ex? Or did she want something more—something Rob wasn't sure he was capable of giving her?

Not that this was about him. It was about her.

'Was the split very long ago?' he asked. If it was recent, still raw, he needed to tread very carefully indeed. The last thing he wanted to do was to hurt someone who'd been so kind and lovely to him.

'Nearly two years since he moved out, and it took a while for the divorce to come through,' she said. 'We wanted different things. It didn't work out.'

Rob was pretty sure there was a lot more to it than that, but he wasn't going to pry. If Florence wanted him to know, she'd tell him. In the meantime, he'd respect her privacy. 'I'm sorry. I've never been engaged, let alone married or divorced, but I know from friends that it can be rough.'

'Yeah. It was,' she said. 'But it's past. I'm over it. Over him. And I like my life as it is. No complications.'

Which told him exactly where he stood. And it was pretty clear to him that she'd offered to let him stay because she'd felt guilty about the way she'd behaved after their night together. She didn't want more. This was her way of making it up to him.

'I agree. No complications is a good thing,' he said.

'But?'

He could bluff it.

Or he could tell her.

Because he was beginning to realise that Florence Jacobs was very clear-sighted. She'd see a problem the way she saw a bit of cross-stitch gone wrong; she'd understand the big picture, she'd untangle things and unpick them, and help him see the way forward. Was she the one who could help him adjust to this new life, the one without most of the things he loved? Could she teach him how to put down roots and not long to be elsewhere?

But he didn't have the words. Not yet. 'No buts,' he said. And, even if she was prepared to help him, she needed to be clear about what she was letting herself in for. 'I was born with itchy feet—and probably my brother's share, too. So complications…aren't helpful.'

'I understand.'

The shutters went right back up in her eyes. Though that was probably a good thing. Rob didn't trust himself to be able to stay away from Florence; he needed her to want to stay away from him, too. Keep herself safe.

'Don't stitch for too long,' she said, moving back to her own seat. 'Apart from the fact that sitting for a long while in one position isn't good for you, stitching for hours will make your hand ache.'

'Got you,' he said. But he wanted to finish the bookmark. Prove to himself that he could do this.

Florence Jacobs was the domesticated sort. And that meant she was the last person he should let himself fall for. Rob wasn't domesticated. He'd never been able to settle. He wouldn't fit into her world. But the more he was getting to know Florence, the more he liked her.

Could he domesticate himself for her?

Though that was assuming that she wanted to be with him, when she'd already made it pretty clear she saw him purely as a colleague. It was an arrogant assumption: and Rob wasn't arrogant. He was impulsive and fidgety, but he didn't think that the world revolved around him.

But all the same, he thought about it.

Particularly during the evening, when he sat and watched a film with her. Unless it was a fast-moving action film, usually he didn't manage to last through a whole film without getting bored and fiddling with his phone. But this time, even though it was the kind of costume drama that would normally bore him rigid within minutes, he discovered that he could actually sit still and pay attention.

What was it about Florence that made him able to do that?

And was it something that could last?

Was Florence Jacobs the person he'd never thought he'd needed by his side—but who actually made his world a much, much better place? Was she someone he actually wanted to commit to, the way Oliver was committed to Gemma? How did you even know when you met that someone? He'd never met anyone he'd wanted to commit to before. Not even Janine.

Was Florence the one?

The questions spun round his head, and he couldn't work out the answer.

'You look all in,' she said quietly.

'I…' Yes. It was probably why he wasn't

thinking straight: he still had a fever. His brain
was scrambled by the infection. And so was
his common sense. 'Sorry.'

'Don't apologise. Go and get some rest. I'll
see you tomorrow.'

Rest wasn't something he was good at. But
he'd try. 'OK. See you tomorrow.'

# CHAPTER SIX

WHEN ROB WOKE, the next day, he felt a lot more human. And it was a reasonable time for a Sunday morning, he was relieved to note when he looked at his watch: eight o'clock. He went into the kitchen, intending to make coffee, and saw a note propped against the kettle, with a door key sitting next to it.

*On early shift. Hope you're feeling better. Text me if you need anything. Help yourself to anything you want for breakfast and lunch, and I'll cook dinner when I get home. Have left you spare door key in case you need to go out. F*

She'd been so thoughtful. He wasn't quite up to going out, but it was good to feel that he had the option and he wasn't trapped.

But then there was dinner.

He didn't want Florence to come home after

a busy shift and feel obliged to cook for him. He wasn't going to offer to cook a roast dinner or anything like that himself, because even when he was fully fit he knew his limitations; but he could arrange a delivery. A couple of minutes looking on the internet netted him the information he needed: the local pub did a delivery service, and the menu was excellent.

He texted her.

Thanks for note. Am feeling better. No need for you to cook tonight—it's my turn to provide dinner. Not going to cook something, but could get dinner delivered from The Golden Lion, unless you know somewhere better?

He added a link to the menu.

Let me know what you want and what time, and I'll organise. R

Should he add a kiss?

No. It'd make her uncomfortable, he decided, and sent the text as it was.

After he'd eaten some toast and had a shower, he tried doing some stitching, but it didn't feel the same as it had when Florence had been there beside him. He flicked through the TV channels, but nothing caught his eye.

Sit and read a book, perhaps? He browsed through her shelves. There were a few medical texts and a scattering of classics, mixed in with some modern novels. He knew from the film last night that she liked costume dramas, and when it came to reading she clearly liked historical romances set in Jane Austen's era. But there was nothing that grabbed his interest.

He looked at the photographs on her mantelpiece. He knew she was close to her family, so he wasn't surprised to see framed photographs of Florence holding three different babies—he'd guess they were her nieces, and from the way she was dressed up it was fairly obvious that it was their christening days—and as bridesmaid to a woman who looked so like her that she could only be Lexy, Florence's older sister. There was a graduation photo with Florence's parents and her sister surrounding her, looking thrilled and proud; an amazingly graceful photo of her sister on stage, wearing a tutu and doing some kind of leap, which he guessed must've been taken by the theatre's official photographer; and a picture of what looked like Florence and Lexy as teenagers in a garden somewhere, laughing and clearly loving being together. It made him smile; he had photos of himself and Oliver like that, too.

He took a closer look at her fridge. It was covered with children's drawings, held to the door by cutesy magnets—everything from acerbic Jane Austen quotes through to pictures of cupcakes. There was the 'ballet-saurus' from her oldest niece that he'd seen the other night, a cat with 'Anna' printed laboriously across the top which was clearly the middle niece's drawing, and a scribble from the baby with 'Darcey' obviously written by an adult on the top. There were also a few group photographs, too; he recognised some of the people as their colleagues in the emergency department, so the snaps had clearly been taken on a team night out.

Others showed Florence posing with a woman he guessed was probably her best friend. Florence clearly liked stately homes and costume museums as much as his mother did. Rob thought for a moment how well she'd get on with his mum; Ollie would approve of her, and his dad would be charmed by her...

And what then?

They'd liked Janine, too. But Janine had wanted commitment he hadn't been able to give. Rob hadn't wanted to settle down with her—and he knew he'd hurt her. Just as he had the potential to hurt Florence. These photographs were proof of exactly who Florence was: someone with roots, someone who had sticking power.

Rob didn't have that. He liked the buzz of new things, of exploring. Which made him the complete opposite of what Florence needed.

OK, so his failed kidneys meant his exploring would be very much limited in the future. Technically, there was no reason why he couldn't try to stay in one place. No reason why he couldn't offer Florence more than just a fling. But he'd never managed to make his relationships last before. What was to say he could do it now? The last thing he wanted to do was start something where she'd end up hurt when he walked away. So, even though part of him thought that Florence might be different—she held his interest, the way nobody had before, and he could be *still*, with her—it wasn't fair to her to take that risk and let her down.

Which meant he'd just have to suppress all of these wayward feelings towards her.

And, much as he hated it, he knew he needed to rest. The more he rested now, the quicker he'd be better, and the quicker he could be on the move again. The quicker he could move out of Florence's flat again. The safer they'd both be.

Still feeling a bit out of sorts, he started up a game of virtual chess with Ollie.

His brother texted back.

Rob, it's Sunday. If you're off duty today, want to come over and play this properly instead of virtually?

Yes. And no. He texted back.

Sorry, Olls, can't do today.

He knew that Ollie would assume he was working and had simply made the chess move during a break.

Maybe next week?

He definitely didn't want to see his twin until he was looking a lot more normal, because he didn't want Oliver worrying about him.

He messaged his mum next.

Just checking in. You and Dad OK? All fine here. Love you. x

His mother replied straight away.

Are you ill?

He lied.

No. Why would you think that?

Had his mother developed some weird sort of sixth sense?

You're sounding soppy.

That made him smile. Of course he did. How well she knew him. He texted back.

Sometimes my job makes me appreciate my family.

Which was true. He wasn't actually at work right now; though he rather hoped she'd take the implication that he was. It wasn't an outright barefaced lie; more of an insinuation.

Having a rubbish shift? Come for dinner tonight. Roast chicken and extra-crispy roast potatoes. Apple crumble and custard.

Things she knew would always tempt him.

But if she saw him like this she'd be horrified and worried sick. Not that he felt like driving—and if he got a taxi she'd worry that he obviously wasn't well enough to drive. He could ask Florence to go with him, but that would lead to such a knot of complications he wouldn't be able even to begin to untangle it. So it was better to stick to bare bones and offer an alternative, just as he had to Oliver.

Sorry. Maybe next weekend?

All right. See you then. Talk to you in the week. Love you. x

I'd better be back to normal by then, he thought.

Love you, too, Mum. Say hi to Dad for me. x

So Rob was organising dinner? Florence was impressed.

Thank you. Food at Golden Lion great. Gnocchi for me, please. About seven? Am calling in at Lexy's on my way home.

The reply came almost immediately.

Perfect. Will arrange. Pudding?

No, but thanks for the offer.

What, you're saying no to salted caramel profiteroles??? Shocking!

She could just imagine him smiling as he
typed. Those stunning blue eyes, flickering
with mischief as he tried to tempt her. That
beautiful mouth… Instead of repeating a polite refusal, she found herself typing back.

Go halves on the profiteroles?

Works for me. *Yum*. See you later. x

This was ridiculous. They weren't actually
dating, even though they'd slept together. And
yet this felt light-hearted and sweet, like an
exchange between people who'd just started
dating each other. Exciting. Full of potential.
He'd even typed a kiss; or maybe that was
just Rob being his exuberant self and she was
overthinking this. Though, for a second, Florence could imagine sitting across an intimate
bistro table from him, reaching across to offer
him a taste of something from her plate…
    Oh, help. She really needed to be careful.

She liked the man she was getting to know and it would be all too easy to fall for him. How could she let herself fall for someone who'd made it clear he wasn't going to be around for long? That was the quickest way to risk having her heart broken again. Stupid. She needed to keep him firmly in the friend zone and resist the temptation to make it anything more. Though the more time she spent with Rob, the more she was starting to think that he'd be worth taking the chance on.

On her way home from her shift, Florence called in at her sister's house for a mug of tea and cuddles with her nieces.

'Aunty Floss, Aunty Floss, look at me doing a pirouette!' Anna said.

'And me!' said Darcey, not to be outdone.

'I'm a ballet-saurus doing a bourrée,' Margot announced, and ran after her sisters on tiptoe, pretending to roar.

'Girls, you're exhausting,' Lexy said. But she was smiling. 'Go and show Daddy your new routines, so I can have five minutes with Aunty Floss.'

'OK. Get the grilling over with,' Florence said when her nieces had scampered away.

'So why did you call off going to the park with us yesterday? Were you on a date with Transition Man?' Lexy asked.

Florence sighed. 'Don't call him that.'

'So you *were* seeing him.'

'Not in the way you think. He's my temporary house guest.'

'Oh? How come?' Lexy looked intrigued.

'Don't get ideas. It's *platonic*,' Florence insisted. 'He was taken ill at work. He thought it might be his body rejecting the donor kidney, but thankfully it turned out to be an infection. So he's staying in my spare room for a few days until he's better.'

Lexy grinned. 'So you're playing doctors and nurses with him? I love it.'

'No, I am not. And also not in the sense *you* mean.' Florence folded her arms and glared at her sister. 'I would've done the same for anyone else on my team, if they'd been in his shoes.'

'But,' Lexy said, 'that doesn't alter the fact that you spent the night with him after your department's Christmas dinner. Or the fact that you really like him.'

'Lexy, that's irrelevant. I'm fine as I am,' Florence fibbed.

'Florence Emily Jacobs, remember what happened to Pinocchio,' Lexy warned. 'I know a fib when I hear it. You're lonely. And you're still letting Dan and his behaviour control you. Otherwise you'd be dating again and finding someone you want to spend time with, instead of locking yourself away to protect your heart.'

'I'm not locking myself away,' Florence protested, even though she knew her sister had a point.

'Transition Man is staying with you, so it's a good chance to get to know him better.' Lexy paused, her eyes narrowing. 'One thing. I get that he's ill, but you've done a full shift today. I hope you're not planning to cook dinner and wait on him hand and foot when you get home?'

'No. He texted me with a menu this morning and he's ordering dinner for us both from The Golden Lion.'

'That's an improvement on Dan—who would definitely be a contender for the World's Most Selfish Man Award,' Lexy said. 'The more I hear about Transition Man, the more I like the sound of him.'

'Don't get ideas,' Florence warned. 'We're colleagues. We might become friends. But he's not going to be around for more than a couple of months, so there's no point in starting anything.'

Lexy sighed. 'I won't nag. Well, not much. But, y'know, if the sex was good…what's the harm in having a mad fling with him?'

'Alexandra! You have *children* about!' Florence said in a scandalised stage whisper.

'They're busy showing Max their latest dance routine. We'll hear the second they're on their way back here and need to watch what we say in front of them,' Lexy said, completely unabashed. 'I know you hate me calling him "Transition Man", but I do think you should consider making him that. It might be good for both of you.'

'No, it wouldn't.' Florence groaned. 'I love you, Lexy, but please can we just change the subject?'

The girls came running back in, then, and of course Florence had to cuddle all three of them, listen to Margot reading a story, praise Anna's drawing and handwriting, and sing nursery rhymes and clap along to songs with Darcey.

She adored every second she spent with her nieces, and was grateful to Lexy for being so generous with her children. But, on the way home, Florence thought again how much she would've loved children of her own. Dan had said he only wanted children that were his own flesh and blood; but had that been an excuse? Considering how quickly he'd accepted being a dad to the children of his new partner, did that mean he thought Florence wouldn't be any good as a mum? And, if so, just what had been so wrong with her?

She shook herself. 'Stop the pity party,' she told herself out loud. 'You're lucky. You're close to Lexy and the girls, you have good friends, and you love your job.'

That was enough.

It would have to be enough.

She walked into her flat to find the table laid ready for dinner, and everything was neat and tidy.

Rob greeted her with a smile. 'Hey. How was your shift?'

Dan hadn't asked her that for years before their split. And she ought to stop comparing Rob with her ex. They were very, very different. 'Fine, thanks. You're looking better today,' she said.

'I feel a lot more human,' he said. 'Did you have a nice time with your sister and the girls?'

'I did. And I have more drawings for the fridge.' She produced them from her bag and swapped them over from the last three. 'I'll put these in a file,' she said, scooping up the ones she'd taken from the display. 'Something for the girls to look back on when they're older—and they'll know that I valued them enough to keep them.'

'That's nice,' he said. 'It's good for kids to

know they're valued. I'm pretty sure our parents have still got every drawing Ollie and I ever did, even the scribbles.'

Rob clearly had a good relationship with his parents and his brother, so he was capable of being a family man. 'Do you want kids of your own, one day?' The words spilled out before she could stop them.

But he didn't look in the least bit offended by her nosiness; and he didn't seem at all thrown by her question. 'I've never really thought about it,' he said. 'I'm looking forward to being an uncle when Oliver and Gemma get round to starting a family—but, given that I'm not great at sticking around, I don't think I'd be a very good dad.'

Which didn't quite answer her question. She hadn't asked if he thought he'd be a good dad; she'd asked if he wanted to be a dad at all. But pressing him for clarification would make things awkward. She shouldn't have asked the question in the first place. Instead, she changed the subject. Their meal arrived, ten minutes later, and she managed to keep the small talk going for the rest of the evening.

One thing she was clear on, though, by the time Rob admitted he was shattered and needed to head for bed: whatever Lexy had suggested, and however tempting she found him, Robert Langley couldn't be her transition man. If Florence let him that close again, she wouldn't want to let him go—and he'd made it plain that he wasn't the sort to stay. And, even if he did stay, how did she know she'd be enough for him? How did she know he wouldn't see the same flaws in her that Dan had seen and leave her for someone else?

She didn't think Rob was the type to cheat—he had more integrity than Dan—but surely he needed someone who shared his wanderlust? Florence didn't want to travel the world or sleep under the stars in the middle of a desert. She wanted a home and a family, a garden and a dog and blissful domesticity: everything that Rob had hinted he didn't want. So it'd be sensible to avoid the heartbreak by keeping him at a professional distance.

On Monday, Florence had a case that made her think about Rob. The way the boy's mother described him was exactly the way Rob had described himself as a child: and the patient had been diagnosed with ADHD. It made her wonder. During her break, she did a bit of research on her phone. The more she read about ADHD, the more she thought it sounded like Rob. And he was bright; if he hadn't struggled academically at school, nobody would've picked it up then.

She'd seen for herself how frustrated he got when he couldn't be up and about, doing things. Maybe this was the root of it. And, if it was, maybe knowing that would help him.

She was still mulling it over when she walked into her kitchen that evening and something smelled gorgeous.

'Perfect timing. Chicken stir-fry, as promised,' Rob said.

How nice it was to have someone actually cook for her. To share: something she and Dan hadn't done for months before he'd walked out. 'Thank you. I feel very spoiled,' she said.

'That was the idea.' He dished up, and sat opposite her.

'This is pretty impressive, from someone who claims he can't cook,' she said after her first taste.

'I didn't say I *can't* cook. I said I don't cook anything that takes more than five minutes,' he reminded her. 'So how was your day?'

'Fine. I was in Minors.' She looked at him. 'Actually, there was a case I think you might find interesting. I had a boy in this afternoon who'd fiddled with his pen when he got bored in class, taken it to pieces and ended up with the spring jammed in his palm. I had to send him to X-Ray to make sure I wasn't going to damage anything when I removed it.'

Rob grinned. 'That sounds exactly like the sort of thing I would've done as a kid.'

Just what she'd thought, too.

'Mum always brings up my first day at school. Apparently, I was at the bottom of the playing field and climbing a tree before the teachers realised what I was doing—and then I fell out of the tree.'

She stared at him in shock. 'That's terrible! Were you badly hurt?'

'Nope. I didn't even have a bruise. Though I did break my arm twice during my time at infant school. Running on ice isn't the most sensible thing to do, and I'm afraid I didn't learn my lesson well enough the first time round,' he admitted.

'So you were the adventurous child in the class?' she asked.

'I was the fidget with a low boredom threshold,' he said. 'For everyone else, the highlight of the day was story time. For me, it was torture. There was nothing worse than having to sit still and listen for what felt like years. I'd far rather have been running round the field.'

'You didn't think about becoming an athlete rather than a rock star, then?'

He looked surprised, then pleased, that

she'd remembered what he'd told her about his teenage band. 'No. One of the teachers thought I needed something to challenge myself, and he suggested I try climbing. I loved it. It was an obvious next step from climbing to joining the mountain rescue team, then think about a career in medicine.'

'I was thinking,' she said. 'You say you've always had itchy feet.'

He wrinkled his nose. 'More than that. I think I got Ollie's share, too.'

'Have you ever thought there might be a reason for that?'

'Such as?'

She looked awkwardly at him. 'This is going to sound a bit rude, so I apologise in advance. The lad I told you about with the spring stuck in his hand, today—you said it sounded like you.'

He frowned, as if wondering where she was going with this. 'Yes.'

'His mum said he has a very low boredom threshold. He's always fidgeting. Very bright.' She looked him straight in the eye. 'He was diagnosed with ADHD, a couple of years back.'

Rob stared at her. 'Are you saying you think *I* have ADHD?'

'I can't really make a clinical judgement because it's not my field. But I was thinking,' she said, 'it might be an explanation for the way you feel. Why you get frustrated quickly. Why you need to move.'

'Nobody's ever suggested...' He thought about it. 'No. I can't be on the spectrum. Otherwise Oliver would have ADHD, too.'

'The siblings of someone with ADHD are more likely to have it, too,' she said, 'but that's not always the case.'

'But Ollie's my twin.'

'I know, but are you actually identical?' She grimaced. 'Sorry. That's a stupid question. But my best friend's brothers look very like each other, enough for people to confuse them, and they're not twins.'

'Actually, that's a fair question. We always thought we were identical, until the transplant. Obviously they had to check, as part of the work-ups, and it seems we have some differences between us in DNA.'

'That's possible?' she asked, surprised.

'There's something called a copy number variant,' he said. 'Normally you get two copies of every gene, one inherited from each parent. But some areas in the genome have up to fourteen copies of a gene, and that's where you can have variations. Plus, as you get older, your DNA changes due to environmental factors. So even if you start off as identical—monozygotic—twins, you're not actually going to be identical by the time you get to later life.'

'I had no idea that was even possible.'

'Neither did we,' he said. 'I don't know enough about the genetic side of ADHD but, if it involves a copy number variant, that might explain why Ollie and I are so different, given we were brought up the same way.' He gave her a rueful smile. 'At one point, I thought there might be something in the whole "good twin, bad twin" thing.'

'There's nothing bad about you,' she said.

It warmed Rob that she'd gone straight to his defence. 'I wasn't fishing, but thank you for having faith in me.' Her theory made sense. A lot of sense. But at the same time it made him feel as if someone had taken the ground from under his feet.

'I can't believe none of us has picked it up before. I mean, OK, it's not the sort of thing we diagnose in the Emergency Department, but Ollie's a GP. And none of our teachers ever mentioned it.'

'If you weren't falling behind in classes, they probably assumed you were…' She stopped.

'A lively child. That's what every single teacher put in every single report. Every single year.'

'It's not a bad thing, Rob. Just a possible explanation.'

Florence was the first person ever to have suggested it. She'd seen something in him that nobody else had ever seen. It made him feel as if she saw him more clearly than anyone had before—and she wasn't judging him. She wasn't pitying him, either. Her brown eyes were full of sympathy and understanding.

'It would explain a lot. Why Mum had to put me on reins as a toddler because she knew otherwise I'd abscond, but Oliver didn't need them because he'd walk nicely. Why I need to climb or just *move*, even as an adult. Why I fidget all the time. Why I can just about sit through an action film, but anything slow doesn't stand a chance.'

'Low boredom threshold, bright, fidgety: it fits,' she said. 'Though I apologise for being—well, intrusive. It wasn't my place to...' She grimaced.

'I don't think you're being intrusive,' he said. 'You've just given me an explanation for a puzzle I'd never been able to solve. Something that never even occurred to me or anyone else.' He looked at her. 'What made you think of it?'

'It's just that everything the boy's mum said

sounded so much like the way you talk about yourself. And it made me wonder.'

'Now you've said it, I can see it.' He shook his head. 'We always assumed it was just me just "being Rob". But there's a reason. Something that isn't a f—' He stopped.

'Isn't a what?' she asked quietly.

Could he tell her the thing that he barely even admitted to himself? Then again, she probably already knew. She saw him more clearly than anyone ever had. Including himself.

Would she turn away from him if he said it? Or would she…? He decided to take a risk. 'Failing in me. Why I've always let women down in the past.'

'Let them down?'

'I'm not a cheat or a liar,' he said. 'But I always seem to pick people who don't want the same things as me. People who wanted me to give up climbing and the overseas aid work.'

'Then I think the failing was in them for expecting you to be something you're not. To expect you to change for them,' she said.

And how weird it was—as if she'd taken a huge load off his shoulders. All the guilt of his past. For the first time, she'd made him see that it wasn't just him.

'You're fine just as you are,' she said.

His mouth went dry. So was she saying she liked him, the way he was starting to like her?

He'd already said more than he'd intended. But he ended up blurting it out anyway. 'I like you, too.'

She went very pink. 'I…'

'That wasn't meant to be any pressure,' he said.

'I know.'

But the air hummed with sudden tension. The things neither of them were saying. The more time he spent with her, the more time he wanted to spend with her. She was like nobody else he'd ever met. But what did *she* want? She'd said before that she didn't want any complications. Did that rule him out? Could he become someone who wasn't complicated?

'Florence, I…' His words deserted him. He'd never had that happen before.

And she let him off the hook by moving the subject back onto safer ground. 'I might be completely wrong about the ADHD,' she said. 'Either way, it's a huge thing to take on. It'd knock anyone for six. Give yourself time to… Well, to let it sink in. Talk to your brother about it.'

All very sensible. And he was supposed to be sensible. Plus, much as he wanted to scoop her up and carry her off and kiss her until they were both dizzy, he was still feeling under par and couldn't actually do it. He'd told her he liked her. He needed to take it slowly and build on that. 'You're right,' he said. 'I will. Seeing as I'm being forced to rest all week, I've got the time to do a bit of research.' He grinned. 'My brother's going to love this. Especially as I talked him into making a pact with me.'

'What kind of pact?' she asked.

'He's going to "be more Rob" and do things outside his comfort zone, and I'm going to "be more Ollie". That way, we're both kind of bringing out the best in each other.' He shrugged. 'It's worked so far. If I hadn't nagged him to be more me, he wouldn't have told Gemma how he felt about her and they wouldn't be together now.'

'So he's kept to his side of the pact. Did you keep to yours?' she asked.

'Of course. The proof is that I'm sitting here right now,' Rob said. 'Being sensible and resting while I'm recovering from the infection.'

'I seem to remember having to pull rank and boss you about to get you to stay here,' she pointed out. 'Which only worked because you were really ill—otherwise I don't think you would've been sensible.'

'I'm trying,' Rob said. 'And that's the best I can do.'

'That's enough,' Florence said. And her smile made his heart feel as if it had done an anatomically impossible backflip.

Florence was feeling decided out of sorts by the time she got home on Tuesday.

'Are you OK?' Rob asked.

'Yes,' she lied.

He simply raised an eyebrow.

She sighed. 'No. I had a case that really got to me today.'

'Want to talk about it?'

'I had a patient who'd gone out to lunch to celebrate her retirement, tripped on the stairs, and smacked her knee on the metal trim of the step.'

'Sounds nasty,' Rob said.

She nodded. 'There was a ten-centimetre laceration under her knee, about two centimetres wide—and it went down to the bone.' Though that wasn't what had upset her. She'd seen far gorier cases.

But Rob seemed to have worked out that talking through the medical stuff was giving her the space she needed to sort out her feelings, because he asked, 'So you treated it as an open fracture?'

'Yes. There was an arterial bleed, too. We managed to stem it, and I gave her prophylactic intravenous antibiotics and sent her for an X-ray to check if there was a fracture. Luckily there wasn't, but I had to send her to Theatre so the surgical team could close the wound.'

'Good call. A wound that deep gives a huge risk of infection,' Rob said.

'I asked her if I could call anyone to be with her, and she said no. No partner, no kids, her sister's in New Zealand, and she didn't want to burden any of her friends.' And that was the thing: would that be how her life was, in thirty years' time? No partner, no children, maybe not living near her sister any more and with the girls having moved away? She bit her lip. 'So I sat with her in my break.'

'That was kind,' he said.

Kind wasn't how she felt. At all. 'Sorry, I'm a bit…' She grimaced. 'I probably need to go for a run. Shake off my shift.'

'You're a runner?'

'It clears my head if I have a case that gets to me,' she said. 'Given that in Manchester you'd actually have to drive somewhere to climb, I'm surprised you're not a runner when you're at work.'

'I am, when I can't climb,' he said. 'I like to run by the canal or the river. Water works when I can't get to climb something. It's not quite as good, but it's better than nothing.'

She smiled. 'I like being beside the sea, when I'm out of sorts. I take the girls and we build sandcastles or look for shells.'

Another vision flashed through Rob's head of three little girls with his eyes and Florence's fine bone structure. The five of them building sandcastles by the sea, finding pretty shells, listening to the waves swishing on the shore...

Oh, for pity's sake.

He'd never had these sorts of fantasies. This was the second time in a week. What the hell was wrong with him?

He needed air.

'You know what? You've had a shift that's left you feeling a bit down, and I think we both need a change of scene. Let's go out for pizza or something,' he said. 'My treat, because it's my idea.'

For a moment, he thought she was going to protest.

But then she nodded. 'Thanks. That'd be nice.'

'You don't have to dress up,' he said swiftly. Because he'd be in real trouble if she looked as incredible as she had at the departmental Christmas dinner. Dressed casually and with no make-up she was gorgeous enough; dressed up, she'd be irresistible. 'Just you and me, pizza and a taxi?'

'No need for a taxi. I'll drive,' she said.

'We'll do some car karaoke, then,' he said. 'Pretend I'm your nieces and sing along with me.'

That, to his relief, made her smile.

And somehow they ended up singing various Abba tracks on the way to the pizza place.

He noticed Florence smiling to herself as she parked the car. 'What?'

'I was just wondering about your teenage band. Which was better, your guitar playing or your singing?'

'Oh, my singing,' he said. 'By a long way. My guitar solos were right up at the screechy end.'

The corner of her mouth twitched. And then they were both laughing themselves silly.

'Sorry. I don't mean to mock you. But...' She trailed off, shaking her head. 'Singing might not be your forte, Rob. I hate to think what your guitar was like.'

'I did say our parents and our neighbours were all over the moon when the band broke up,' he reminded her, and grinned. 'Ollie can't sing, either. Imagine the pair of us doing harmonies round the house. You should've heard our version of "Bohemian Rhapsody".'

She grinned back. 'Well, hey. Nobody's perfect.'

'You're right. By the way, you sing flat, too. Though not *quite* as flat as I do,' he allowed.

It broke the tension between them, but when they were settled at their table in the pizza place Rob found himself wishing that this was a proper date.

Florence had said she was over her ex, but was she really? Did he stand a chance with her? He'd been trying to tell himself he should stay away; but the pull he felt towards her was so strong.

Then he became aware that she was asking him something.

'Sorry. I zoned out temporarily. Lack of carbs,' he fibbed, not wanting to tell her what he'd actually been thinking about. 'Would you mind repeating that?'

'I was just wondering how your research was going,' she said. 'The ADHD stuff.'

Brilliant. So he could avoid the emotional stuff he found it hard to deal with. 'It's hugely interesting,' he said. 'I went through some questionnaires, based on what I was like as a kid and how I am now.'

'And?'

'It looks as if I'm pretty much a textbook case,' he said. 'And it's probably why I like emergency medicine: everything's fast, I know what I'm doing and I thrive on—'

'—pushing yourself too hard,' she finished.

And it explained why his relationships had fizzled out in the past. He got bored quickly and he wasn't good enough at paying attention to his partner's needs. And he suspected that both his brother and his parents had accommodated his behaviour because he'd never got into real trouble at school and he'd never struggled academically. Everyone had just assumed that he was a bright boy with a low boredom threshold. Rob the Restless. Rob the Risk-Taker. It had been good-natured teasing: but maybe if he'd had a clue earlier he might not have hurt past girlfriends by not being there enough for them. At least he knew what to watch for now.

'So where do you go from here?' she asked.

'I'm meeting Ollie for lunch tomorrow,' he said. 'I thought we'd throw a few ideas about.' And, given that Oliver was so happy with Gemma now, maybe he could point Rob in the right direction with Florence, too...

Florence was glad that they hadn't bothered ordering wine, on the grounds that she was driving and Rob was on antibiotics. She needed to steer well clear of anything that might lower her inhibitions even a fraction in the vicinity of this man.

He was good company. Charming, warm and funny.

He was beautiful, too.

And he kissed like an angel.

But he also thought he wouldn't make a good dad, which meant he probably didn't want children. So she'd just have to keep reminding herself that he was Mr Wrong.

# CHAPTER SEVEN

ON WEDNESDAY, ROB took a taxi to Ashermouth Bay and met his brother outside the surgery.

'You look terrible,' Oliver said, giving him a hug. 'Have you been overdoing things?'

'No. I just had a bit of an infection. The antibiotics are working nicely, and I'm on the mend now,' Rob said.

'What? An infection? When did this happen? Why didn't you tell me?' Oliver demanded.

'Because you'd worry, you'd tell Mum, and she'd fuss.' Rob clapped his brother's shoulder. 'Stop worrying. I'm fine. *Really.* I felt a bit rough on my shift last week, and I was sensible about it and went to the renal department. No misplaced heroics.' Even though originally he had intended to wait until after the end of his shift, Ollie didn't need the worry of knowing that. 'They ran all the checks, decided it was an infection rather than the beginning of rejection, and gave me some meds.' He grimaced. 'And they signed me off for a week.'

'Why didn't you come and stay with me?' Oliver asked.

Rob squirmed. 'Look, I've already wrecked one engagement for you. I didn't want to wreck this one, too.'

'Apart from the fact that it wasn't your fault Tabby ended things, and Gemma isn't Tabby—Rob, for pity's sake, you're my *twin*. Next time something like this happens, you call me,' Oliver said, glaring at him. 'Yes, of course I'll tell Mum, because we need to keep her in the loop so she doesn't worry herself stupid, but I'll also be a buffer and make sure she gives you the space you need.'

Rob blew out a breath. 'Sorry. I know I probably should've said something earlier.'

'There's no "probably" about it,' Oliver said.

'I just didn't want to worry you. Or get in the way with you and Gemma.'

'You wouldn't get in the way. Gemma seems to like you, for some strange reason,' his twin said dryly.

'I like her, too. She's right for you,' Rob said. 'So, where are we going for lunch?'

'Pub?' Oliver suggested.

'Can we get a quiet table?' Rob asked. 'I'd like a bit of advice.'

'That sounds serious.' Oliver's eyes were full of concern.

'It's absolutely nothing to do with the infection or the transplant,' Rob reassured him.

Once they were seated and they'd ordered, Rob said, 'So, the advice stuff. As a GP, how would you go about diagnosing a patient with ADHD?'

'Why?'

'Humour me,' Rob said.

'All right. I'd start with talking to my patient's parents, go through the diagnostic questionnaires with them and maybe with the school with the parents' permission, then do a referral to a paediatrician specialising in spectrum cases.'

'What about if the patient was an adult?' Rob asked.

'Then I'd go through the diagnostic questionnaires with them. Why?'

'Has it ever occurred to you,' Rob asked, 'that *I* might have ADHD?'

'No. You're just you.' Oliver looked thoughtful. 'Though, now you've said it, you certainly fit the hyperactive side of the criteria. Mum always says you were the busiest toddler she's ever met. But we're identical twins, and I don't fit any of the criteria: so how can you have ADHD if I don't?'

'Because we're not *quite* identical,' Rob said. 'Remember when they tested us before they did the transplant? Bits of our genomes are different, which is why they put me on low-dose immunosuppressants. I've been reading up a lot about the copy variant stuff, this week, seeing as I've been off work—'

'—and you can't sit still and rest,' Oliver interjected.

'My point precisely,' Rob said. 'And it's possible that we're a bit more different than we thought.'

'So you think you might have ADHD.' Oliver looked him straight in the eye. 'Are you asking me to diagnose you and maybe prescribe something, Rob?'

'No, to both,' Rob said. 'I'll see my own GP for a proper diagnosis. I just wanted to know what you think. And apparently there are other ways to deal with it, not just medication.'

'A lot of undiagnosed adult ADHD patients self-medicate to manage how they feel,' Oliver said. 'Actually, now I think about it, that's what you do.'

'What? How?' Rob frowned. 'You know I've never abused prescription meds or taken any kind of drugs. I don't smoke. And, although I appreciate good red wine, I stick to the limits.'

'That's not what I mean,' Oliver said. 'And not even your chocolate habit. It's the risky stuff you do. The climbing. The humanitarian aid stuff. I think that's how you manage yourself.'

'So are you saying that, if my GP put me on meds, I wouldn't need to climb any more?' Rob asked.

Oliver shook his head. 'I think climbing means too much to you for you ever to give it up. And you'd need to discuss treatment with your GP. But if my hunch is right and climbing's what you do to manage it, then you need to find something to challenge you until you're fit enough to go back to climbing. Something you can do while you're resting and healing.'

'I might have done that,' Rob said, thinking about the sewing and Florence. 'Or, rather, a friend might have found the answer.'

'Friend?'

Of course his twin would pick up on that. They knew how each other's minds worked and often finished each other's sentences. Rob wrinkled his nose. 'It's complicated.'

'You don't do complications.'

'I know. But I kind of want to.' He sighed.

'Which is even more of a complication, and I don't have a clue what to do about it. Where to start.'

'Be honest with her. Talk to her,' Ollie said. 'Don't keep stuff back.'

'The ADHD? She was the one who suggested it. There was a boy in the department with a spring stuck in his hand.'

Oliver grinned. 'That sounds like the sort of thing you would've done at school.'

'Yeah,' Rob admitted. 'The more she talked to the boy's mum, the more she thought he sounded like me. So she asked me if I'd ever considered it.'

Oliver thought about it. 'That makes a lot of sense. The way you need to be on the move all the time. The fact you're such a minimalist— if you don't have any clutter in the first place, that means you can't get overwhelmed by it. The way you hyper-focus, whether it's work or climbing or anything else you do. Actually, that makes you pretty amazing, because you've worked out how to deal with it all by yourself, without even knowing what the problem is in the first place.'

'I did get a fair bit of help,' Rob corrected him. 'Remember the teacher who got me into climbing?'

'That's a good point,' Oliver said. 'He'd

probably seen quite a few kids who couldn't settle and discovered that the discipline of climbing helped them.' He frowned. 'I wonder why he didn't talk to Mum and Dad about it and suggest having you tested?'

'Maybe he did and they said no, I'd always been a busy child, and it was just a phase I was going through. Not that I'm criticising them,' Rob said swiftly, 'just trying to make sense of things.'

'Back then, ADHD and Asperger's weren't really understood,' Oliver mused. 'We still don't know enough about the spectrum, but back then a child who couldn't pay attention and never got homework in on time would've been labelled lazy—nobody would've thought about teaching them time management.'

'I never handed my homework in late,' Rob said. 'Though I did zone out in a couple of exams. The teachers assumed I was distracted by girls.'

'Which was also fair,' Oliver said, 'considering the number of them who fell at your feet.'

Rob shrugged. 'Right now I feel a bit of an idiot for not realising before why I was different.'

'Talk to your GP. Get the official diagnosis. And,' Oliver said, warming to his theme, 'you're right about stuff other than meds being able to help. For a start, there's exercise.'

Rob raised an eyebrow. 'Climbing?'

'Not just that. Something you can do anywhere. Gemma and I have been sorting out stuff for our elderly patients.'

Rob gave him a speaking look. 'I'm ten minutes older than you, not four decades.'

'I don't mean that. I meant the stuff we've been putting on the practice website about exercise for health. Mental as well as physical. There's yoga.'

Yoga—which Rob knew Florence did every week. Could he do yoga with her?

'A one-to-one teacher would probably be more helpful than a class for the mindfulness stuff. I found something called mindful walking, the other day, but I haven't got round to researching it properly yet. I'll add it to my list and see if it's something that might work for you.' Oliver smiled. 'And I'll do any or all of it with you, if you feel too self-conscious or weird to do it on your own.'

'Thank you, because right now I feel a bit stupid for not realising it before.'

'You're very far from stupid, and you're not the only one who should've picked it up.' Oliver clapped his brother's shoulder. 'We've got this. And you need to talk to your friend. Tell her how you feel about her.'

'What if she doesn't feel the same way?'

Oliver coughed. 'We've had this conversation before. Except it was me with the doubts, last time. Take your own advice. Talk to her and be honest.'

'But how do you know, Olls? When you meet The One?'

Oliver looked at him. 'It's that serious?'

'Answer the question.'

Oliver sighed. 'I got it wrong with Tabby, remember.'

'Yes, but you've got it right with Gemma. How did you know?'

'She made me feel as if the sun was shining every time she walked into the room,' Oliver said. 'The doubts were all in my head. If I'd be enough for her—because I wasn't enough for Tabby.' He looked at Rob. 'What's her name?'

'Florence.'

'How does she make you feel?'

'Still,' Rob said. 'I can be *still*, with her. It's...' He shook his head. 'But she's been let down, and I've never wanted to commit to anyone before. There's always been a mountain to climb and a world to conquer.' He paused. 'What if I hurt her? I can't trust myself to commit.'

'The old you—before the kidney—would never even have considered that,' Oliver said.

Rob flinched. 'Because I'm selfish and unthinking.'

'No. You were always honest and you never pretended to be anything you weren't,' Oliver said. 'But you sound different. You sound as if you want something else now.'

'I do.' And that particular revelation still shocked him. 'But, when I'm fully fit again, will I be like I was before?'

'Restless? I don't know,' Oliver said. 'But having to be still and wanting to be still are two very different things. One of them is your choice.'

'I guess.'

'How does Florence feel about you?'

'I don't know,' Rob admitted. 'I think she likes me.'

'That's a good start.' Oliver paused. 'The only way to find out is to talk to her.'

Talking. Which he was great at when it came to putting patients at their ease, and rubbish at when it came to relationships. But he knew his twin was right.

'What are you doing?' Florence asked, the next morning, when Rob walked into the kitchen wearing his work suit.

'Going to work. If you don't mind giving me a lift, that is.'

'I do mind,' she said. 'You were signed off for a week.'

'It's been *nearly* a week,' he said.

'Six days.'

'What's one little day between friends?' he asked with a smile. 'And I feel perfectly fine.'

'You're pushing yourself,' Florence warned.

'I'll pace myself. I promise,' he said. 'But I need to be back at work. I need to feel I'm doing something.'

'You were signed off for a week,' she repeated.

'And I'm feeling back to normal,' he said. 'It's Thursday. I'm not due in tomorrow. If I go in today, it eases me back into things.' He gave her a rueful smile. 'To be precise, it eases me back into the schedule that's meant to ease me back into things.'

'If you feel the slightest bit rough,' she said, 'then you say so and you *stop*.'

'I will. Promise,' he said. 'For me, believe me, this is taking it slowly.'

'Hmm.' But she drove him in.

And it was fine until the middle of the afternoon, when the paramedics brought in a young mum-to-be who'd been in an accident.

\* \* \*

'This is Kelly. Thirty-four, five and a half months pregnant with her first baby, and she was rear-ended in a queue of traffic,' the paramedic told Florence and Rob. 'The airbag didn't go off, but she's worried because she can't feel the baby moving.' She lowered her voice. 'I couldn't pick up a heartbeat with a stethoscope, but that could be the way the baby's lying.'

Florence really hoped she was right.

The paramedic spoke normally again. 'No sign of contractions, no leaks of any kind of fluid, and obviously Kelly's worried so her pulse rate is a bit on the high side.'

Some good news, some not so good. 'OK. Thanks. I'll get a call up to Maternity,' Florence said quietly, and turned to her patient. 'Kelly, I'm Dr Jacobs and this is Dr Langley. I know right now you're feeling scared, and we're here to look after you and the baby. Before today, did you feel much movement?' With a first baby, Florence knew the mum might not even feel the baby moving until around twenty-four weeks.

'A bit. It felt like fluttering.' Kelly was pale. 'But there's been nothing since the crash.'

'That doesn't necessarily mean there's a problem,' Rob reassured her. 'Babies all have different rhythms. Are you booked in with the team here?'

'No, I live in Glasgow. I just came over for the day to see my gran. I… Oh, God.' She bit her lip. 'I can't lose this baby.'

'Can we call anyone for you?' Rob asked.

She shook her head. 'My partner's on his way. And my mum's called Gran to say I…' Kelly shuddered, and her words ground to a halt.

'That's fine. He'll be here soon,' Florence said soothingly. 'We'll give you an ultrasound scan so we can see how the baby's doing.' And so she could check the placenta; an impact, even if the jolt wasn't that severe, could make the placenta shear away. 'I'll examine you as well, if that's OK.' She took Kelly's hand and squeezed it. 'I know right now everything feels incredibly scary, but you're in the best place.'

Kelly was shaking and crying too much to reply.

Please let the baby be all right, Florence begged silently. And she was glad Rob was here. He was the perfect person to help her, right now. Those blue eyes and that smile of his would go a long way towards helping calm Kelly down.

'Do you know your blood group?' Rob asked.

'A positive,' Kelly said shakily.

Florence exchanged a glance with Rob. That was one complication they could avoid, then. If Kelly had been Rhesus negative, there was a risk that if the baby was positive and the baby's blood mixed with hers, Kelly's immune system might become sensitised and attack the baby's red blood cells. Rhesus disease was the last thing Kelly needed right now.

'That's good,' Florence said. 'Do you have any pain—anything that feels like a bruise, or any feelings of tightness?'

Kelly shook her head. 'I don't... I can't... just... Please, is my baby OK?' she begged.

'I'm going to get the portable scanner now,' Florence said. 'I'll be gone for five minutes tops.'

'And I'm going to stay right by your side,' Rob said, his voice full of reassurance. 'Try and breathe slowly for me—three counts in, three counts out—and I promise that will help with all the scary stuff. I'll count you through it. Count along in your head with me. And that's in, two, three...'

Florence knew she was leaving Kelly in the best possible hands. Rob was excellent with patients, calm and kind. He'd be the perfect anchor. Once she'd closed the curtains round the cubicle, she grabbed the first person she saw. 'Ranj, I've got a woman in from an RTA. It's her first pregnancy and she can't feel the baby move. Can you grab someone from Maternity, and tell them it's urgent? Rob's with her now and I'm getting the portable scanner.'

'I'm on it,' Ranj said.

'Thanks.'

She wheeled the scanner through to the cubicle. 'How are you doing?' she asked.

'The baby's still not moving,' Kelly whispered.

Please, please let this be just panic and a first-time mum not yet used to feeling her baby's movements, Florence begged silently. Please let it all be OK.

She gave Kelly a reassuring smile, and talked her through what she was doing as she set up the scan.

'We wanted this baby so much,' Kelly said. 'It took us three attempts at IVF. All I want is to be a mum—and this is all my fault. If I hadn't come to see my gran, then I wouldn't have had the accident.'

'It's absolutely not your fault,' Florence reassured her. 'Apart from the fact you were stationary when the other driver hit you, accidents happen anywhere.'

Florence knew it was true, but it put a lump in her throat. This could so easily have been her, if Dan had agreed to try for IVF with a sperm donor. She knew how it felt to be so desperate to have a baby. The waiting and the hoping and the disappointment that grew sharper every month.

That little catch in Florence's voice right now: Rob was pretty sure something was very wrong indeed. Had something like this happened to Florence, and maybe her ex hadn't been supportive enough?

He glanced at Florence, but her expression was that of a concerned doctor; the woman was hiding behind the job. Though he noticed a moment of anguish when Florence stroked the transceiver head across Kelly's stomach. 'I can see the baby's heart beating,' she said, and turned the screen so Kelly could see it for herself. 'Look. The baby's kicking. And the heartbeat's there. Nice and strong.'

Kelly sobbed in relief, and Florence held her hand tightly. 'It's going to be all right,' she soothed.

Though that wasn't strictly true. Rob could see a blood clot on the screen—something Florence clearly wasn't making a big deal of it because it would terrify their patient. It looked to him as if Kelly might have a concealed placental abruption, where the blood was trapped between the wall of the womb and the placenta rather than showing as a vaginal bleed. He exchanged a glance with Florence and knew her clinical judgement mirrored his.

'Kelly, may I examine you?' Florence asked gently.

'Yes, of course.'

'No sign of blood or any tears,' she said.

But then Kelly said, 'My back aches a bit now. I didn't really notice before, because I was so scared about the baby and that's all I could focus on.'

'What kind of ache?' Florence asked.

'Like when you catch the back of your hand on the corner of a desk and about three days later it's sore,' Kelly said.

Like a bruise. That definitely wasn't a good sign, Rob thought.

'I'm going to ask someone to come down from the maternity department to see you,' Florence said carefully. 'It might be that they decide to keep you in overnight and keep an eye on you, because the symptoms you're describing mean it's possible that a bit of your placenta has come away from the wall of your womb.'

'My placenta's come away?' Kelly's face paled. 'Is my baby going to be OK?'

That depended on the severity of the abruption, but Rob knew they needed to keep Kelly as calm as possible. 'We'll do our very best to keep your baby safe,' was the best he could promise.

Ranj came in to tell them that Naz Mahmoud, one of the senior registrars from the maternity unit, was on her way down. A couple of minutes later, Naz arrived and Florence had a quiet confab with her outside the cubicle to fill her in on the situation before bringing her in to introduce her to their patient. 'Naz will look after you now, Kelly. All the best,' Florence said.

'You're in good hands,' Rob reassured her.

He intended to grab Florence and whisk her off to the hospital canteen for a coffee and a quiet chat, to see if she was OK, but the red phone shrilled again with news that the paramedics were bringing in someone with a suspected stroke; there just wasn't time to leave the department.

'Are you OK?' he asked.

'Of course,' she replied.

He knew she wasn't telling the truth, but right then there was nothing he could do to help.

At the end of their shift, when their patient with a stroke had been admitted, Florence said, 'Give me ten minutes before I give you a lift?'

'Sure. I'll get some hot chocolate to go. Meet you by the car?'

'Thanks.'

Whenever was upsetting her, it went deep. And Rob knew he was going to have to tread very carefully indeed to make sure he didn't make things worse.

When she met him at the car, she was all smiley and chirpy. And Rob could see straight through the act. 'Hot chocolate,' he said. 'And cake.' Cake made everything better. 'Do you want me to drive?'

'No, it's fine. Thanks for the hot chocolate.' She took a sip, almost as if she was trying to prove to him that she was fine, then slid the cup into the holder in her car.

Rob fell back on the doctors' old trick of waiting for the patient to fill the silence. But, with Florence also being a doctor and knowing the same trick, it backfired on him; she didn't say a word. And she had that brittle smile on her face all the way into her flat.

He knew he wasn't great with emotional stuff, but no way was he going to abandon her. 'I'll cook. There's pasta in the fridge and a pot of sauce.'

'I'm not hungry,' she said.

'You've had a tough shift,' he said. 'And you're not okay. Florence, I'm a guy and I'm not great at talking about feelings, but even *I* can see you're upset, and I'm pretty sure that it's to do with Kelly. Talk to me. I'm here, and it's not going any further than me.'

When she still said nothing, he sighed. 'Just ignore the fact I'm six feet tall and male. Imagine I'm your ballerina sister,' he said, 'because I think you really need a hug.' He wrapped his arms round her and held her close. He wondered if she was going to pull away again, or if she'd actually talk to him.

And finally he felt the tears judder through her.

He rested his chin on Florence's shoulder and kept her wrapped in his arms until she'd managed to stop shaking. Then he settled her at the kitchen table and made her a mug of tea. 'Talk,' he said. 'Was it Kelly?'

She nodded. 'Naz said we were right. It was a concealed abruption. Kelly was asleep when I called up.'

'Rest—' much as he hated it personally '—can do a lot.'

'Yeah.'

Why had this case got to her so much? Had something like this happened to her? He knew he'd be twitchy if they had someone in with a burst appendix or a transplant rejection; he'd be cool and calm in the department, but afterwards—when he was on his own and had had time for it to sink in—it would definitely get to him.

'Forgive me for asking,' he said softly. 'I don't mean to hurt you or bring back bad memories. But is that what happened to you? You had an abruption and lost a baby?'

She swallowed hard and whispered, 'I didn't even get that far.'

He remembered what else Kelly had said: she'd had IVF. 'You had IVF that didn't work?' he guessed.

Florence shook her head; when she looked up at him, her huge brown eyes were filled with pain.

He didn't understand. 'What can I do to help?'

'Nothing.'

He couldn't just sit here and watch her suffering.

He scooped her out of the chair, sat her on his lap and held her close. He could feel her shaking with the effort of trying not to cry.

'No judgement,' he said softly, 'and nothing you tell me will go anywhere. Just the same as you haven't told anyone about me and my kidney.'

'I told the head of the department I'd taken you to the renal team.'

'That's different. The head of the department already knew about my kidney, and it's the kind of thing that managers need to know.' He stroked her hair. 'If you don't want to talk, that's fine. But sometimes getting the words out stops things hurting quite so much.'

She was silent for so long that he thought she was going to close off on him.

But then she sighed and rested her head on his shoulder. 'Dan—my ex—we tried for a baby for three years. When we didn't get anywhere, we saw our GP and went for tests. I was fine but Dan wasn't. There was a problem with his sperm; he had a really low count and the motility was poor.' She bit her lip. 'Apparently he had mumps when he was about thirteen. Nobody paid any attention to it at the time, but clearly that affected his fertility.'

'So IVF didn't help?'

'It might've done. But he absolutely refused to do ICSI, where they'd extract his sperm under a microscope and inject it into my egg, or IVF with donor sperm.' She closed her eyes. 'I desperately wanted a baby, Rob.'

But her husband had been infertile; and he'd refused the medical treatment that could have helped. She'd said the divorce was because they'd wanted different things. Now he was beginning to understand.

'I'm sorry,' he said, stroking her hair. 'That's tough.'

'And that poor woman today… It could so easily have been me, if Dan had agreed to the IVF.'

They were taught to maintain professional distance at work, but every so often a case resonated with you. Really hurt. Clearly this was one of those for Florence. 'Just remember, you were there to help her. You got her admitted so she's under close observation.'

'There's no guarantee the abruption won't get worse and she could lose the baby.'

'There's no guarantee the abruption *will* get worse,' he said gently, 'and if it does she's in the right place to get the help she needs immediately, and that'll make all the difference. You did your bit, Florence, and you *helped.*'

'It doesn't feel enough,' she whispered.

Her misery felt bone-deep and he ached to comfort her. 'It's enough. *You're* enough.'

'It doesn't feel it,' she repeated.

Had this affected her so personally that it made her doubt her own medical judgement?

Before he could find a way of asking her and reassuring her, she said, 'It's not just that he refused IVF or adoption. He said they wouldn't be his kids biologically.'

'It takes more than biology to be a parent,' he said, furious that the guy could've been so selfish and hurt her so much. 'And I'm sorry he let you down.'

She looked away. 'It turned out that he did want kids, after all. Just not with me. He— he had an affair. And he didn't have a problem with his mistress already having kids who weren't biologically his. He just didn't want kids with me.'

Rob bit back the harsh words that rose to his lips. She didn't need his anger. She needed comfort.

'Because there's obviously something wrong with me,' she finished.

'There's absolutely nothing wrong with you, Florence Jacobs. You're bright, and you're kind, and you'd make a brilliant mother. Any man would be proud to love you.' That included him. Though he'd never talked to her about love, and now absolutely wasn't the time. How could he tell her that he was more than halfway to falling in love with her, and he didn't have a clue what to do about it because he'd never felt like this about anyone before? 'He didn't value you the way he should've valued you, and that's *his* fault, not yours. Never yours.'

'Thank you.' But she still didn't look as if she believed him. He didn't know what to do, what to say. He just held her close.

And he meant to give her a reassuring kiss on the cheek; but somehow their mouths connected.

Somehow his eyes were closed.

Somehow he was really kissing her, as if they were both drowning and needed each other for air…

And then she broke the kiss and slid off his lap. 'My head's not in the right place for this.'

He'd stepped so far beyond the boundaries, it was untrue. 'I'm sorry, Florence. That wasn't… I shouldn't have done that. I was trying to… I don't know, show you how much I want you. That you're *enough* for me. I got it wrong, and I apologise.'

'It's not you. It's me.' But she wouldn't meet his gaze.

'It's *not* you,' he said. He paused, feeling awkward. 'Look, I understand if you want me to go. I'll get my stuff together and call a taxi.'

'No—it's fine.'

But it wasn't. It wasn't fine at all. 'I…um— look, let me cook you that pasta.'

'I'm not hungry,' she said. 'I just need an early night.'

'I'm so sorry.' It was very English, he thought: apologising, apologising for apologising, and both of you going round in circles while you stuck up a protective wall. And he didn't know how to deal with this. How to make it better.

'Not your fault.'

'Can I—? Do you want a drink of anything?'

'You already made me tea.'

Which she hadn't drunk and there was a skin forming on the top.

Anything he said now would just make things worse. 'If you need anything…' Oh, and how did that sound? Of course she didn't need him. Mr 'I can't commit, and I blame it on my itchy feet when it's really just my own failings'.

She just gave him a wan smile. 'Nobody in the department knows—about…'

The words were clearly sticking in her throat. 'They won't hear anything from me. It's nobody else's business,' he reassured her. He rather wanted to pay her ex a visit, dangle him off a narrow ledge and make him admit what a worm he was. But that wouldn't solve anything. 'See you tomorrow,' he said.

But he sat up late, thinking.

Now he knew the truth about her marriage

break-up, it proved that, even though he was falling for her, he wasn't the right one for her. She wanted children, and he'd never been in a relationship to the point of wanting to settle down and have children. Florence Jacobs wasn't like anyone he'd dated before; but he wasn't dating her. She was his temporary colleague. Until tonight, he would've said they were becoming friends. But he'd made things awkward between them, responded in completely the wrong way.

He was only staying with her until he recovered. And he should've left a couple of days ago, when he'd started feeling better. He shouldn't have given in to the temptation to stay. Shouldn't have responded to her warmth. *Shouldn't have kissed her again.*

Was she asleep? Probably not. But he could hardly knock on her bedroom door and ask to talk to her. Quietly, he packed his things. Tomorrow, he'd get a taxi to the hospital, pick up his car, and go…well, not home. Back to his flat.

And he'd have to be bright and breezy with her in future. Treat her as nothing more than a colleague, not even a friend. It wasn't want he wanted—he wanted *her*—but he couldn't give her what she needed. She deserved a chance to find someone who'd love her, someone who'd give her the family she dreamed of.

And how he wished it could've been him. That he was different. But if he stayed, he'd let her down, and she'd already been let down enough.

The next morning, she'd clearly decided on the same tactics, because she was bright and breezy with him. 'Toast?'

'Thanks, but I'm fine,' he said. 'And I wanted to say thank you for looking after me so well, this week.'

'You're very welcome. You look a lot better,' she said.

'I feel a lot better,' he said. 'So it's time I got out from under your feet and went back to my own flat. I've stripped the bed and put everything in the laundry basket. I've got a taxi booked for—' he glanced at his watch '—any minute now, so it makes sense for me to wait outside. I'll see you at work on Monday.'

'OK.' She gave him a super-bright smile that didn't fool him in the slightest. He knew she felt just as awkward as he did. But she'd been the one to call a halt, and he wasn't going to push.

Back at his flat, he contacted the local florist and arranged for a hand-tied bouquet to be delivered, with a message.

*Thank you for looking after me. You were a good friend and I appreciate it. Rob*

And then, with nothing better to do, he cleaned his flat. Twice.

The flowers were spectacular. Large roses, spray roses and stocks, all in delicate shades of pink, set off with pretty foliage.

Florence knew who they were from before she opened the card.

Pink. He'd chosen that deliberately. Like the flowers she'd taught him to stitch.

But the message made her heart sink.

*Thank you for looking after me. You were a good friend and I appreciate it. Rob*

It was perfectly polite—and very distant.

Which was her own fault. She'd been the one to call a halt when he'd kissed her, last night. He'd been comforting her when she was upset. That sweet, gentle kiss on the cheek had been comfort. And she'd kissed him back on the mouth. Instigated it. Stopped it. Given mixed messages.

Of course he'd backed off.

How could he possibly have stayed here after that?

Never had flowers made her feel so miserable.

And her flat felt so empty, without Rob. For the last week, she'd been sharing her space and she'd enjoyed not coming home to an empty flat. To sharing the cooking—well, in his case he'd organised a takeaway, made a very quick stir-fry and taken her out for pizza. But sharing her space. Sharing her time. Getting to know what made him tick. The sewing lessons. She'd loved every minute of it.

Now he'd gone, it felt as if all the colours had dimmed.

She blew out a breath. The flowers were lovely. And she needed to thank him.

Quickly, she tapped a message into her phone.

Thank you for the flowers. They're stunning.

Had they been just a polite thank-you? Or was he using them to try and connect with her again? Should she say something about the sewing, maybe even tease him a little? Would that get their connection back, or would it make him back away even more?

Or perhaps she was overthinking it. In the end, she finished with a safe:

See you Monday.

He didn't reply.

Which told her the flowers had simply been polite. If he'd wanted to take their relationship further, then he would've used the excuse to keep the conversation going. Weeks ago, Lexy had advised her to ask him out. To tell him her dating skills were rusty and suggest maybe going for a drink after work.

But she'd pushed him away. And she'd told him the whole story about Dan, about how she'd so desperately wanted a family. Rob had made it clear that he was only here for a few more weeks. He was leaving. And, even though Florence thought she might be halfway in love with him, she knew that wouldn't be enough to make him want to stay. She hadn't been enough for Dan and she wouldn't be enough for Rob. So she'd stick to being colleagues and having professional boundaries.

But her flat still felt empty. And she couldn't even go and spend time with her sister, because Lexy would ask her about Transition Man and she'd have to explain what a mess she'd made of things.

\* \* \*

Nothing felt right. Nothing distracted him. He couldn't even lose himself in research.

And that text Florence had sent him was so polite it set Rob's teeth on edge. 'See you Monday' clearly meant 'Please don't contact me over the weekend'.

If only he could go climbing.

A walk on the beach didn't help much, because he remembered she'd said she liked the sea when she was out of sorts. He liked water, too, but this time it didn't help.

Nothing helped.

And he didn't have a clue how to make things right with her.

If only he'd kept his mouth to himself. If only he hadn't given in to the impulse to kiss her. That was where it had all gone wrong. He should've just comforted her, moved out over the weekend so he was ready to go back to work, and then asked her out.

But no.

He'd kissed her.

And she'd told him straight that she wasn't interested.

He managed to get himself in full charm mode for lunch with his parents, Oliver and Gemma on the Sunday. His twin insisted that they keep the tradition of the two of them doing the washing-up, though Rob knew it was an excuse for Oliver to grill him.

'So did you talk to Florence?'

He couldn't admit, even to his twin, how badly he'd messed up. 'No.'

'That advice you gave me was sound,' Oliver said.

'Yeah.' No, it wasn't. 'I'll talk to her.'

And if Oliver knew it was a big, fat fib, at least he also knew not to press it.

# CHAPTER EIGHT

IF THE WEATHER was meant to reflect your mood, Monday morning should've been filled with endless rain and fog. But of course it was sunny, with the sun sparkling on the frost. Rob scowled, and stamped through the corridors. Somehow he had to regain his equilibrium before he saw Florence again. Treat her as if she was just another colleague, when she was actually the first woman he'd ever wanted to settle down with.

By the time he reached the double doors to the department, he'd managed to put a professional smile on his face.

The bit he was longing for and dreading in equal measure was seeing Florence. How would she be with him? He'd take his cue from her, he decided. His conversation with Ollie had clarified things in his head: he wanted her to see him as someone safe. Someone who wouldn't let her down. And he needed to find a way of doing that—once he was sure that was what she wanted, too.

The roster showed that they were in Resus together. Which meant they'd have to work closely, but at least they'd be busy and completely focused on their patients. At least that was one area where they were in tune.

The red phone shrilled, and Florence's face was grim when she put it down again. 'Builder, forty, fallen ten feet off a ladder. The paramedics say his GCS was ten at the scene, dropped to eight, and he's had a seizure and isn't communicating. His partner's on his way in.'

With any fall from that height, Rob knew, there was a worry about head injuries; and the seizure hinted that there might be a possible bleed in his brain, which would need surgical intervention.

They set up, ready to receive the patient. Once the paramedics had brought him in, between them they lifted the patient off the trolley and onto the bed, leaving his neck brace in place. There was blood trickling from his nose and his left ear; Rob caught Florence's eye, seeing the slight worry in her face. Like him, she recognised it as a sign of potential problems.

She shone a light in his eyes. 'Pupils equal and reactive,' she said.

That was better news, Rob thought.

He could hear the man whispering. 'What's happened? Where am I?'

'You're at the hospital,' he said. 'You fell off a ladder and we think you hit your head. I'm Dr Langley, and this is Dr Jacobs. We'll be looking after you.' He paused. 'Can you remember your name?'

'Tim,' their patient said. 'My head hurts.'

Conscious, talking and lucid. That was a really good sign, even though the pain in his head might not be.

'Tim, we're going to send you for a scan and see what's going on,' Florence said, holding his hand. 'Your partner's on the way in.'

A tear trickled down Tim's face. 'Can't move my head.'

'You've got a neck brace on to protect your spine,' Rob said. 'Once we've done the scan, we'll know if we can take it off.'

'Ash will kill me. Said be careful, it's icy.'

'These things happen,' Florence said gently. 'He'll be here soon. And we're here to look after you.'

The scan showed pockets of air in Tim's skull.

'I don't like this,' Florence said. 'I'm going to call the neurologist to review the scan.'

'Good call. Looks like a possible fracture,' Rob said. 'And large pockets of air can compress the brain. I've seen that in people who fell when cl—' He stopped, realising what he'd just been about to say. Given what his favourite occupation was, that wasn't tactful. And it wasn't the way to convince Florence that he was a safe bet; it'd make her think he was someone who'd fill her future with worry.

'Climbing,' Florence finished. 'And you wonder why your mother worries about you.'

Yeah. She knew he'd cause her worry. 'I wear a helmet.' Wore. Who knew when he'd get the chance to climb again? 'And I don't climb in poor conditions,' he added, to make sure she'd understand that he was restless, not reckless. There was a difference.

'Good.'

But she didn't meet his eye.

How was he ever going to get things back to normal between them? How was he going to persuade her to give him a chance?

'I'll do a couple of checks on Tim while you call the neuro team.'

'And I'll go and find his partner on the way back to join you,' she said.

Thankfully Tim seemed even more lucid

than he had earlier, and Rob was able to reassure him a bit and run through a few checks before Florence and Tim's partner joined them.

'Ashir, this is Dr Langley, who's helping me look after Tim. Rob, this is Ashir, Tim's partner,' Florence introduced them swiftly.

Ashir shook his hand. 'Thanks for what you've done.' Then he turned to Tim. 'So falling ten feet off a ladder is your idea of being careful?'

'Could've been worse. Could've been twenty feet,' Tim said.

'I'm glad you're talking. When I got that call, I thought...' Ashir shuddered and held his partner's hand.

'You always said I was bone-headed,' Tim said, clearly much more relaxed now his partner was here.

'I swear I'm going to glue that safety helmet to your head in future,' Ashir said.

It was the same kind of banter he'd started to have with Florence, when he'd stayed with her. And it made his heart ache that it wouldn't happen again.

Later that morning, the neuro team admitted Tim for observation, but a second scan had been more promising.

'Watch and wait,' Florence said.

Was she going to tease him about 'wait' being his second-favourite four-letter word? Rob wondered. But she didn't. And that threw him. They'd become friends over the last few weeks. If she didn't even see him as that, how could she ever see him as anything more? He wanted her to see him as more. He'd been thinking about it for days.

And he didn't know how to reach out to her.

'Come over for dinner,' Oliver said on Wednesday evening. 'You sound as if you could do with Gemma's lasagne and some cake.'

'Hang on—you're starting to appreciate cake now?' Rob teased.

'Gemma's a cake fiend. I have no choice,' Oliver said. 'Seriously, though. You sound a bit low. And it'll be more fun than sticking something in your microwave.'

'Yeah.' And maybe his twin would have some insight into how to fix this impasse with Florence. Something other than 'talk to her', because Rob knew he'd already made a mess of that.

He called in at the supermarket on the way to his brother's, buying flowers and wine. Gemma was at a dance aerobics class—though Rob could smell the lasagne bubbling in the oven.

He was halfway through explaining the situation with Florence to Oliver. 'I want to prove to her that I can stick at something,' he said.

At that moment, Gemma came into the kitchen, kissed Oliver hello and hugged Rob. 'Hey, Rob the Risk-Taker—planning your next climb?' She tried to ruffle his hair; when that didn't work, because his hair was so much shorter than Oliver's, she laughed. 'Sorry.'

'No, you're fine.'

'Tell Gem what you were telling me,' Oliver said. 'She has the advantage of two X chromosomes, so she understands how women's minds work.'

'What can I do to help?' Gemma asked.

'I feel a bit bad, talking about someone else's private life,' Rob said.

'It's not going any further than us,' Gemma said. 'Talk.'

Rob explained about how Florence had been hurt before and didn't want to take any risks. 'And with me being what I am…' He grimaced. 'She's the first woman I've ever felt like this about. I need to find a way to prove to her that I'm serious about her.'

'Try telling her exactly what you just told us,' Gemma said.

'Words aren't enough. I need something physical.' He thought about it. 'She likes needlework. She taught me to do cross-stitch. Maybe I can make her a picture.'

'That's not something you can do like snapping your fingers, Rob,' Gemma said. 'Even a bookmark, if you did a proper one with a few different colours and backstitch, would take you about ten hours—plus unpicking the bits where you've gone wrong, because everyone has to unpick things.'

'I know I've got a reputation for being impatient—' Rob began.

'You *are* impatient,' Oliver interrupted.

'But I can be patient for this. I can focus. Because it's important.' He spread his hands. 'I guess there's a benefit to only working three days a week, after all: it means I have time to do it.'

'Putting your feelings in stitching instead of words. Well, that'd definitely show you mean it and it isn't just a whim,' Gemma mused. 'Though don't stitch all day without a break, or your hand will hurt for a week.'

'She said something like that when she taught me how to stitch,' Rob said wryly. 'And you sound as if you know about stitching.'

'I know a bit because my best friend Claire's mum Yvonne has a craft shop. She runs workshops and I sometimes help out. What do you want to make?'

'I don't know,' he admitted.

'She'd be an excellent person to ask for ideas, plus she can sort out what you need to make whatever it is when you decide,' Gemma said. 'When are you free next?'

'Tomorrow,' Rob said.

'Right. I'll call her tonight and tell her about you. Meet me at the practice at lunchtime and I'll introduce you to her,' Gemma said.

'Thank you, Gemma.'

She smiled. 'You're welcome. That's what family's for. Well, I'm not *quite* family.'

'You're engaged to my brother. You make him happy. You're definitely family,' Rob said, and hugged her.

'So that's the thing she did to challenge you? Taught you to sew?' Oliver asked.

Rob knew his twin wasn't mocking him. 'Yes. It's weird. I would never have believed it would work.'

'Counting stitches. I guess it'd have the same effect as counting reps at the gym,' Gemma said. 'Mentally, that is. Not physically.'

'It's weird,' Rob said again.

'What I can't get my head round is that it means you actually sit still. That's almost unheard-of,' Oliver said with a smile. 'I know how much you miss climbing, and I'm glad you've found something that grounds you. Better still, something that doesn't involve dangling off a mountain.'

'I'm trying to be more Ollie,' Rob teased.

'Yeah? There's one thing that pact of yours doesn't take into account,' Oliver said.

'What's that?'

Oliver patted his arm. 'I love you for who you are. You're worth the risk. If she understands you, she'll get that.'

'I hope,' Rob said, 'you're right. Because at this precise moment it feels impossible.'

'Think of your climbing,' Oliver said. 'You'd do a risk assessment and work out how to scale a crag. This is the same thing.'

'He's right,' Gemma said.

Except, if he miscalculated this, the hurt would go much deeper than just a broken bone...

The next day, Gemma introduced him to Yvonne, and he explained what he wanted. 'This is what she taught me to do,' he said, and brought out the bookmark. 'I want to sew something for her that tells her I love her.'

Yvonne drew up a file of photographs on her laptop. 'There are a few patterns here. There's this one.'

A heart, filled with rows of different sorts of hearts. It was pretty, but… He shook his head.

'It's pretty, but it's generic. I want something personal.'

'OK. Give me a bit more detail. What do you want to tell her?'

'That with her I'm not restless any more. I can be still.'

Yvonne thought for a bit. 'So she makes you feel grounded, as if you have roots?'

'That's it exactly.'

She scrolled rapidly through the file of patterns, and brought up another one: a tree, whose trunk was made out of the word 'love' in a very fancy script; the branches made a heart shape, and the leaves were hearts. 'How about this?'

'It's almost perfect,' he said. 'How do you add something to a pattern?'

'It depends what you want.'

'I want the tree to have roots that spell out her name.'

Yvonne put a hand to her face. 'Oh, that's so romantic! Well, I can tweak the pattern for you. Do you have a laptop and a printer?'

'Yes.'

'Then I'll sort it out for you over lunch and email you a PDF,' she said. 'Now, I assume you need the fabric, threads and everything else?'

'Yes, please.'

'Come and see me when it's done, and I'll frame it before you give it to her. On the house, as you're Ollie's brother and Gemma's like family to me.'

'Thank you,' Rob said. And he called in to the chocolate shop on the quayside on his way home, choosing a special assortment to be delivered that afternoon to thank Yvonne for her help.

He started work on the project as soon as he got back to his flat. He knew it would take time and he couldn't rush it, but hopefully this would show Florence what was in his heart. Tell her what she meant to him. Prove to her that he could manage his itchy feet, with her by his side.

And then maybe she'd agree to try to make a go of things with him…

On Friday, they were both rostered in Resus.

And again, Rob was aware of the awkwardness between them.

He'd never wish ill health on anyone, but he was glad of their first case, that morning: Michael Winters, who'd been brought in by his grandson.

'Grandad wouldn't let me call an ambulance,' the young man said. 'He just didn't look right this morning. I checked his pulse and it was sky-high, and his breathing's not good, so I bundled him in the car and brought him in.'

The triage team had sent them straight to Resus.

'Good call,' Florence said. 'How long has your grandad been like this?'

'Since I saw him this morning. Maybe overnight—I was late in, last night,' he said.

'Has he ever had anything like this before?' Florence asked.

'Not as far as I know, though I could check with my dad.'

'Are there any medical conditions we need to know about?' Rob asked.

'If stubbornness is a medical condition,' the grandson said wryly, 'he's definitely got it.'

Rob was very aware of Florence looking straight at him.

Was she calling him stubborn, too? She was one to talk.

'Nothing,' the young man said. 'He doesn't smoke. He likes his glass of whisky before he goes to bed, but it's not a huge one. He takes the dog out every day, and he eats properly because I live with him and I do the cooking.'

'OK. We'll assess him now,' Florence said,

'so if you don't mind waiting in the waiting room, we'll come and get you as soon as we've finished.'

The young man nodded. 'Do what they tell you, Grandad,' he said, squeezing Michael's hand. 'I want you back home with me. And I want you well.'

'You fuss too much, Dylan,' Michael wheezed.

Rob wasn't happy with Michael's heart rate—more than double the norm—or his oxygen saturation levels.

'Oxygen,' he said to Florence, 'to help with his breathing.'

'And beta-blockers,' she said, 'to get his heart rate down.'

The longer the over-rapid heartbeat went on, the more stress it put on the ventricle, the lower pumping chamber of the heart, and it could lead to heart failure.

But the beta-blockers and oxygen seemed to have no effect, and Michael complained of feeling sweaty.

'I think we should do cardioversion,' Rob said.

'Agreed,' Florence said, looking grim.

'I'll go and have a word with Dylan.'

He found the younger man in the waiting room.

'Is everything all right?' Dylan asked.

'As you know, your grandad's heartbeat is too fast—something called superventricular tachycardia or SVT for short. There are lots of different causes for it,' Rob said. 'The most common one is an electrical problem with the heart. We'll be able to sort that out, but for now we need to get his heart back into a normal rhythm and he isn't responding the way we'd like to medication. So we want to give his heart a small electric shock.'

'But—isn't that what you do when someone has a heart attack?'

'Sort of,' Rob said. 'What it'll do is bring his heart back to a normal rhythm. It'll only take about ten minutes. Your grandad will be under sedation so it won't hurt; he might feel a bit dizzy afterwards and might have a little bit of chest pain, but we'll keep him in for a few hours on the cardiac ward to keep an eye on him. The cardiac ward can also run tests to find out exactly what kind of electrical problem caused the SVT and how to treat that so he doesn't get this again.'

'Just make him better,' Dylan said. 'Whatever it takes.'

'I'll come and get you when we've done it,' Rob promised, and headed back to Florence. Between them, they sedated Michael, put the sticky pads on his chest and attached the electrodes to the defibrillator.

Things might be a bit strained between them personally right now, Rob thought, but they were in tune at work.

'And clear,' Florence said, and administered the shock.

The results were dramatic: from the scary one hundred and eighty-five beats per minute, Michael's heart rate dropped straight down to a more normal seventy-five beats per minute.

'Result,' she said. 'Go and fetch Dylan, and I'll ring the cardiac team to get Michael admitted.' She smiled. 'It's good to have a good outcome.'

'Definitely,' Rob said.

And if only he could make sure that things between himself and Florence had a good outcome, too…

# CHAPTER NINE

IN THE MIDDLE of the following week, Florence had to drag herself out of bed when her alarm went off.

Maybe she was going down with some kind of bug; as a morning person, she never usually struggled getting up for work. Washing her hair didn't make her feel any better. She made herself a mug of coffee, but couldn't quite face drinking it because the smell made her feel slightly queasy; and her toast tasted odd. Metallic.

Some viruses affected your sense of taste and smell, she knew. If she was going down with something, the last thing she wanted to do was to spread it among her colleagues.

She checked her temperature; it was normal.

But she still didn't feel right.

She was about to call work, saying that she felt rough and didn't want to spread whatever it was, when it hit her: she hadn't bought any tampons for more than a month.

And her periods were normally so regular that she could practically set her watch by them.

She counted back swiftly. Her last period had been just before Rob had started at the hospital, and her current period had been due on the week that he'd stayed with her. She'd been so busy concentrating on fighting her attraction to him that she hadn't noticed her period was late.

She wasn't sure whether she was more excited or apprehensive. Three years ago, she would've been trying to contain her excitement—and at the same time wary of getting her hopes up, only for them to be dashed again. Now... Now, she wasn't even in a relationship. And the idea of being pregnant was terrifying. Her whole life would be tipped upside down.

Could she be pregnant?

Or maybe she was overthinking this. Maybe because her routine had been slightly disrupted, her body had followed suit and she'd just skipped a period.

Although the night she'd spent with Rob had been smack in the middle of her cycle, her most fertile time, they'd used contraception. OK, so a condom could fail; but even if that was the case, she knew that he was also taking immunosuppressant drugs to stop his body rejecting his brother's kidney. It wasn't her area of medicine, but she was pretty sure she'd read studies showing that immunosuppressants affected fertility.

Which meant the chances of her conceiving were infinitesimally small.

Sipping a glass of water made her feel a bit better.

And that in itself was worrying. The symptoms were all starting to point away from a bug and towards...

Oh, help.

She didn't have time to worry about it now. She'd be late for her shift, if she didn't get a move on. She pulled herself together and headed for work. And she was seriously glad that Rob was off duty that day, because she couldn't have handled working with him—not with this weighing on her mind.

Thankfully they were so busy that she didn't have time to think about it during her shift; but there was only one way to prove to herself that her missed period was just a blip, caused by a change in routine or stress or whatever. She couldn't be pregnant.

Once she'd done her handover, she drove to

an out-of-town supermarket, put a magazine in her shopping basket and then slid a pregnancy test underneath it, so if she did bump into someone she knew they wouldn't see the test and jump to conclusions.

She knew the drill and she was pretty sure that this test would be the same as every one that had broken her heart when she and Dan had been trying for a baby and her period had been a couple of hours late. When she'd taken a test, full of joyous anticipation, hoping that this would be the month their dreams would come true. She'd pee on the stick and wait for a minute; the line would show up in the first window to say the test was working; and then...

With every test, the other window had stayed stubbornly blank. And each one had sucked away a little more hope, until the point where they'd gone for testing. They'd expected that the problem was hers; the doctor had dropped the first bombshell, but Dan had dropped the bigger one.

She shook herself. That was then. This was now. And the test would just confirm that of course she wasn't pregnant. She performed the test, set the stick on the sink on the ledge between the taps, washed her hands, and glanced at the stick. It was all exactly as she expected:

one window with a line to show that the test was working, and one blank window.

So she wasn't pregnant.

She stared at herself in the mirror. 'See? You were just being paranoid and stupid and ridiculous. Of course you're not pregnant.'

She knew she should have felt relieved. But she felt the echo of all the failed pregnancy tests from before, and it made her sad. She'd thought her life would be so different. That she, like her sister, would find it easy to get pregnant. That she and Dan would have children. Be a family.

There was nothing wrong with being single. You didn't have to have a partner and children to be fulfilled. She had a family she loved, a job she loved, good friends.

Except, deep down, she was lonely. Sharing her flat with Rob for a week had reminded her that she enjoyed living with someone else.

Though Rob had made it clear that person wouldn't be him. That he didn't want to settle down.

Tonight, she decided, she'd start looking for a flatmate.

She was just about to wrap the test and drop it in the bathroom waste bin when she realised that the second window had changed when she wasn't looking. It wasn't blank any more.

There was a line. A faint line, but it was definitely there.

She stared at it.

No way. This had to be some kind of mistake.

She blinked, and stared again. The line was still there. And now her certainty deserted her. Did that mean it was a positive test—or was it a false positive? Was she actually pregnant, or was it just a hormonal blip?

If she was pregnant, then she'd need to tell Rob. He had the right to know that she was expecting his baby. But she had no idea how he would react. Would he decide he had to do the right thing, and then resent her for trapping him? Or would this make him want to leave even faster?

When she'd asked him if he wanted kids, he'd said he thought he'd be a terrible dad. But would he really? Children needed to know they were loved. Rob was impulsive—but he'd been unfailingly good with their patients, paying attention and listening to them. The way he spoke about his family left her in no doubt that he loved them dearly. She was pretty sure he'd love their child.

What she wasn't sure about was how he felt about her. He'd comforted her when she'd let that case get to her—but then it had turned to kissing. So was it just all about the sex? And was that enough for a relationship? Or would she fail as badly as she had with her marriage to Dan?

Though she could hardly call Rob and talk to him right now, not when she wasn't certain.

Even two and a half years ago, the prospect of doing a second test to check it was a definite positive and not a mistake would've filled her with elation. Right now, she just felt confused: as if her world had tilted and she was sliding towards the edge.

Pregnant.

A baby.

The thing she'd wanted so much for so long, and thought wasn't possible.

Wasn't the saying, be careful what you wish for?

Because now it looked as if she might have her wish.

She wanted a baby. She wanted a child with a deep, visceral longing. Yet, at the same time, she was terrified. Being a parent wasn't easy; being a single parent was even harder, even though she knew her family and friends would be there for her.

Right then, she didn't have a clue what to do.

She could call Lexy—of course she could— or her mum. They'd both support her.

But Rob was the one she wanted to talk to most. And, until she was absolutely certain it wasn't just a blip, a false positive, she couldn't call him.

The obvious thing to do now was a second test. She headed back to the supermarket, and this time bought a different test—the all-singing, all-dancing sort that could be done even before you missed a period and told you in writing how many weeks pregnant you were. And this time she bought a double pack, in case something went wrong with the first test.

Back at her flat, her chest felt tight and she could hardly breathe.

And she couldn't squeeze out a single drop of urine to do the test.

She drank a glass of water. Paced up and down her flat. Waited. And she still didn't need to pee. 'Oh, for pity's sake. Don't be so wet,' she told herself. She made herself a mug of coffee, on the grounds that caffeine irritated the bladder and made you want to pee more quickly. This morning—and in fact all day at work—she hadn't wanted coffee; but, if need be, she'd hold her nose so she could drink the stuff. She added enough cold water so she could drink it straight down, and paced the flat again. Yet still she didn't have the slightest urge to pee.

It was driving her crazy. She needed to know the answer, and she needed to know now. Was she or wasn't she pregnant with Robert Langley's baby? Just how long did it take liquid to go through your system? Was this how Rob felt all the time, twitchy and edgy and scattered? How did he cope, short of heading up the nearest mountain?

'Argh,' she said. Distraction. That was what she needed. Something to take her mind off it. Sewing was usually her answer, but this time she couldn't concentrate. She kept thinking of Rob when she'd taught him to sew: his beautiful blue eyes, his nearness, how she'd been tempted to steal a kiss. And that really, really, wasn't helpful.

OK. Chores, then. She vacuumed the living room, then glanced at her watch. Surely more time must have passed than that?

What next?

Maybe some yoga would help her settle. She tried some of the moves she'd learned at class, but they didn't help. She couldn't concentrate. Not until she had the answer.

Then finally, finally, she was ready to take the test.

Every nerve-end prickled. Would it be positive—or would it be negative?

She took a deep breath, did the test and capped it. As before, she left it on the ledge of the sink while she washed her hands. She could feel her pulse speeding up as she waited for the result to show; or did her pulse only feel faster because the seconds were dragging?

A line appeared in the first window, so the test was definitely working.

Now for the bit she needed to know. Pregnant or not?

She wasn't aware that she was holding her breath until the words actually appeared on the screen; and then the noise that came out of her mouth was the kind of wail that shimmered between joy and despair, everything all mixed up together.

She was pregnant. More than two weeks. Which fitted with her dates and the night she'd spent with Rob.

She sank down on the floor, drew her knees up to her chin and wrapped arms round her legs.

What now?

One thing she was definite about: she was keeping the baby, whatever happened. All those years of longing meant there was no way she'd choose a termination or to carry to term and have the baby adopted. This baby might not be planned, but he or she would most definitely be loved. She knew her family would support her and so would her friends.

But she had to tell Rob that she was expecting his baby.

It was the kind of conversation they needed to have face to face. Even a video call wasn't good enough. She didn't want to leave any room for misunderstandings.

She grabbed her phone and texted him.

Need to talk to you about something. Are you free this evening?

He didn't answer immediately, but she tried not to be unreasonable about it. He might be busy doing something with his brother or his parents. His phone might be accidentally on silent so he wouldn't know he'd got a text; or it might not even be switched on at all. The battery might have run out. There were all kinds of reasons why he wasn't answering.

There was still no answer after half an hour.

This wasn't something that could wait, because it would weigh on her mind. Though it was definitely not something she wanted to discuss at the hospital.

She'd have to bite the bullet and call him.

Taking a deep breath to calm herself, she went into her contacts list and pressed on his name. She could feel her pulse accelerating as the line connected; but after two rings the call went to voicemail. She waited for the beep to leave her message. 'Rob, it's Florence Jacobs. I'd appreciate it if you could call me this evening, please. It doesn't matter what time. Thanks.'

Then she groaned when she ended the call; she must've sounded so snooty. *Florence Jacobs.* How many Florences would he know? But she could hardly call back and gabble something else now.

'Robert Langley, you are the most annoying man in the universe,' she muttered. 'Why is it so hard to get hold of you?'

It could be hours until he returned her call. And she needed to eat—for the baby's sake, if not her own. Plus she needed to work out what she was actually going to say to him. She made herself an omelette, grabbed a pen and paper to make notes about how to tell him, and just taken the first bite of her dinner when her phone rang and Rob's name flashed up on the screen.

She gulped the mouthful down and hit 'accept'; but the food went the wrong way so she was coughing like mad when her phone connected.

'Florence? Are you all right?'

She swallowed a mouthful of water and coughed a bit more. 'Yes.'

'I just got your message,' he said.

'OK.'

'You asked me to call you. Which I'm doing.'

'Thank you.' But everything she'd meant to say went out of her head. Why hadn't she written it down before she'd even called him the first time?

'Florence? Are you still there?'

'Uh…yes.'

'What did you want?'

She took a deep breath. 'I need to talk to you about something.'

'I gathered that.' She couldn't tell if he was irritated or amused. 'I'm listening.'

'I… Not on the phone.'

She could practically hear the frown in his voice. 'Are you all right?'

That rather depended on your perspective. 'Yes.'

'Then what…?'

He sounded confused. Yeah. She knew how that felt. 'Can we meet?'

'Do you want me to drive over to you?'

'No. I'll come to you.' If, when she told him

the news, and he decided that he didn't want to be involved—which was what she was expecting—then at least she could walk away with her head held high, rather than be the one left behind.

'What time?' he asked.

'I'll leave now. See you in a bit.' She ended the call and forced down the rest of her meal; then she brushed her teeth, stuck the pregnancy test in an envelope and the envelope in her handbag, and drove over to his flat.

The only time she'd been to his flat before had been the day he'd come to stay with her. She hadn't taken in their surroundings as he'd packed an overnight bag.

Bearding the lion in his den. Or would Rob be a lamb rather than a lion?

She had absolutely no idea how he was going to react to her news. He'd kept his distance from her over the last week or so, not even suggesting grabbing a coffee or lunch together on the days when they were both rostered in Minors. So did that mean he'd back away even further when she told him about the baby?

There was no point in trying to second-guess him. And as for how to tell him… She was beginning to think that the best way was to be blunt.

She flicked on the stereo, and switched it off when she recognised the song as one of the ones she and Rob had caterwauled along to, the day he'd taken her out for a pizza when she'd been feeling low after her shift. He'd teased her into a brighter mood, and they'd laughed until they'd hurt.

It had felt so right.

But then it had gone so wrong…

She parked outside his flat. There weren't butterflies fluttering in her stomach; it felt more like a stampede of panicking dinosaurs.

She rested her hand on her stomach. 'You can do this, Florence Emily Jacobs,' she told herself. Then she hauled herself out of the car, walked up to the entrance to the block of flats, and pressed his intercom button.

He answered immediately. 'Hi, Florence. I'll buzz you in.'

And he met her at the door, looking concerned. 'Can I offer you a drink?'

'No, thanks.'

'OK. Come and sit down.'

His flat was super-neat and very minimalist; there was almost nothing on any of the surfaces, other than some framed photographs on the mantelpiece. It felt more like a show flat than a home.

She perched on the edge of one of the chairs.

'So what did you want to talk to me about?' he asked.

'There isn't an easy way to say this.'

'Say what?'

Oh, God. Why hadn't she practised this? In the end, the words came blurting out. 'I'm pregnant.' When he said nothing, panic filled her. 'I'm telling you simply because you have the right to know, but I don't expect anything from you.'

He still said absolutely nothing.

Which told her everything. He wasn't interested. And she couldn't take him rejecting her the way Dan had. She needed to leave. Now.

'That's all,' she said, and stood up. 'I can manage everything on my own, so don't worry that I'll demand anything from you. It's fine.'

She was pregnant.

With his baby.

Rob couldn't think straight.

He'd had no idea what she might want to talk to him about. His focus over the last few days had been entirely on trying to work out how to persuade her to take a chance on a proper relationship with him.

Now she was telling him she was expecting his baby.

He shook his head to clear it; it didn't work.

But then she stood up, ready to walk out of his life.

He couldn't—wouldn't—let that happen.

'Florence. Don't go,' he said. 'We need to talk about this.'

'There's nothing to say. I know you don't want kids.' She shrugged. 'It's not a problem.'

'No,' he said. 'That's not true. I've never said I don't want kids. And I don't…' He shook his head. 'Please. Don't go. Let me process this. Let me get my head straight so I don't say something stupid. And if I do say something stupid, cut me a bit of slack. Because all it means is the words are coming out wrong.'

For a moment, he thought she was going to leave anyway.

But then she nodded.

'Can I get you some cof—?' He stopped, mid-offer. Were pregnant women meant to avoid coffee? Would the smell upset her? 'Tea? Water?'

'No, thanks. I'm fine.'

'Forgive me for pacing. I'm not— It's not you, it's *me*,' he said. 'I need to move about when I'm thinking.'

'OK. I get that.'

To his relief, she sat down again.

He took a deep breath. 'First of all, are *you* all right?'

She looked surprised, as if she hadn't expected him to think of her welfare. 'Yes. At least, I think I am,' she qualified. 'I'm still getting my head round this.'

'So when you did find out?'

'This morning. It's not like me, having to drag myself out of bed.'

'No.' He looked at her. 'Then what?'

'My toast tasted funny. I didn't want my coffee.' She took a deep breath. 'And I realised my period was late. Normally it's really regular.'

'So you did a test at work?'

'After work. I bought one on the way home. And then I went out for another one.'

He raised an eyebrow. 'Why?'

'The first was just to prove to myself that I was being ridiculous. I couldn't be pregnant. Apart from the fact we used protection, you're on immunosuppressants with your kidney, so that affects your fertility—doesn't it?' She frowned.

'I don't know. It wasn't even an issue at the time,' he said. 'I was single when I went abroad. When they offered me the transplant, my focus wasn't on when or if I planned to start a family with a girlfriend who didn't exist, it was on getting fit enough to work again and be able to go climbing. So, actually, I'd need to look at the meds I'm on and check the details.'

She looked at him. 'So if you're on meds that don't affect your fertility...'

'...and the condoms in my wallet, even though I'm pretty sure they were in date, were old,' he said, 'then that would explain it.'

'With the first test, the line was very faint,' she said. 'It was the first time I'd ever actually seen a line appear in the second window.'

He remembered what she'd said about trying for a baby for years with her ex, and discovering that he was infertile. The disappointment every month when her period arrived must've been crushing—and even more so on the occasions when it had been late.

'I couldn't be sure it was a truly positive result, and I couldn't tell you about the baby unless I was absolutely sure. So that's why I went out and bought a second test—and a spare, just in case.'

Rob wanted to wrap his arms round her and hold her close, tell her that everything was going to be all right; but he knew that he needed to resist the impulse. Right now he needed to give her the space to tell him what was in her head.

'And this time the line was stronger?' he prompted.

'This time it was one of those that actually say it in words, and how many weeks pregnant you are.'

That night was the only time they'd slept together. 'So, if that night was in the middle of your cycle, then you're six weeks now?'

'Yes.' She took an envelope out of her bag. 'The test says three weeks plus. But I calculated the same as you did.'

He took the envelope, removed the test stick and stared at it.

Something he'd never thought he'd do.

And, instead of making him feel trapped and as if he'd been stuck in a little box, it filled him with joy. Pure elation.

They were going to have a baby.

He wanted to pick her up, twirl her round and cheer.

But she—despite the fact she'd told him that she dearly wanted a baby—didn't seem to be very happy about it. Had she changed her mind about babies? Or was *he* the problem?

He needed to know what was in her head. And there was only one way to find out. He damped down all his impulses, and asked, 'So we've established we're having a baby, next summer. What do you want?'

'I already told you, I'm not going to make any demands on you,' she reminded him.

'Leave me out of the equation for now,' he said. 'I want to know what *you* want. Do you want the baby?'

'Yes.'

'And to make a family?'

'I keep telling you, I don't expect you to do anything.'

So did she want to be with him, or not? He was going to have to ask her straight out. And he was probably going to have to be the one to tell her that he wanted to make a go of things between them, because if she *did* want to be with him she clearly didn't want to be the first to say it.

He gave her a wry smile. 'My nickname in the family is Rob the Risk-Taker. This is the one time I really, *really* need to take a risk— and I'm absolutely terrified. Will you promise you'll hear me out and not back away?'

'I...'

'Please, Florence,' he said. 'It's important.'

Finally she nodded. 'All right.'

'So here's the thing. I don't have a proper diagnosis yet, but thanks to you picking it up I think the fact I can't settle is all down to the way my brain is wired, and not just pure selfishness on my part, which makes me feel a bit better about it, but...' He took a breath. 'I'm babbling. What I'm trying to say is that now I know I'm going to be a dad, and that changes everything. I'm absolutely terrified that I won't be very good at it—but I'll do my best to learn *how* to be a good dad, because even though I haven't had much time to get my head round the news I'm thrilled.'

Disbelief was etched across her face. What didn't she believe—that he was going to try to be the best father he could be, or that he was thrilled with the news?

He tried again. 'I know we've done this the wrong way round. You're supposed to date someone, then sleep with them, then decide you want to make a family together. We still haven't even got round to dating properly. We slept together and we made a baby. But things have changed for me since I met you,' he said. 'For the first time in my life I've met someone who actually makes me want to settle down. Someone I can be *still* with. Someone who understands me.'

She still didn't look convinced. Then again, now he knew what her ex had done, how he'd denied Florence her dearest wish and then rubbed her nose in it... 'Your ex,' he said softly, 'is an idiot who didn't recognise what he had with you, and I hate the way he treated you. I have my faults, but I promise I won't ever deliberately hurt you or deny you. I love you, Florence.'

'You love me?' She still didn't sound as if she believed him, but was that a glimmer of hope he could see in her eyes? He'd take that for the win.

'I love you,' he said. 'We haven't known each other for long,' he said, 'but it's been long enough for me to know. I *like* you. The doctor I see at work who's kind, who listens to her patients and takes the trouble to wash someone's face or sit with them in her lunch break because she knows they're lonely. The woman who saw I was ill, and who looked after me without making me feel shut in and smothered. The woman who fitted together the pieces of a puzzle I would never have managed to solve for myself. The woman who taught me how to just *be* instead of having to move all the time.'

'That's liking, not love.'

'I haven't finished,' he said. 'Because I believe liking's the basis of real love. My parents like each other as well as love each other. Ollie and Gemma like each other. And I really like who you are. I like the way you can be brisk and efficient—but at the same time you'll take the trouble to stitch a picture of a dinosaur in a tutu for your niece just because you know she'll love it.

'I like the way you kiss like an angel and you don't mind that I sing flat—you laugh with me, not at me. I like *you*. But, more than that, you make my pulse skip a beat when you smile. Those huge brown eyes of yours turn me to mush. And every time I see you I want to kiss you until we're both dizzy.'

Her eyes glittered with unshed tears.

'And I'm growing to love you a little more every day. I've been going crazy, this last week, trying to work out how to tell you how I feel about you without making you run a mile.'

'But you've avoided me at work.'

'I've been trying to give you space,' he said. 'I was kind of hoping you'd miss me and then I could show you how I feel about you. That I'm serious.'

'Show me?'

'I finished this tonight.' He headed to the sideboard, took the thing he'd been working on all week out of a drawer and handed it to her. 'This is for you.'

Florence stared at the piece of material.

Rob must've been working on the cross-stitch for *days*. It was way too complicated for a beginner.

And it was absolutely beautiful: a tree,

whose branches were in the shape of a stylised heart. He'd added heart-shaped leaves to the branches; the trunk contained the word 'love' in a fancy script; and the roots also made a name.

*Her* name.

'That's amazing,' she said.

'I made it for you,' he said, 'to try to tell you how I feel about you. You ground me, Florence. You're my roots. And what's growing is love.'

Tears filled her eyes. 'I think that's the nicest thing anyone's ever said to me.' Or done for her. She couldn't believe he'd made something so beautiful.

'I mean it,' he said. 'I did have some help finding the design and customising it—Ollie's fiancée is very close to the owner of the local craft shop, and she helped me. But it's from my heart.'

'It's stunning. I can't believe you've put all that work into it.'

'And sat still for so long,' he said with a wry smile.

'It's amazing.'

'So here it is,' he said. 'I'm not offering you something easy. I'm always going to have a restless side, even though now I know what's behind it I can do more to keep that under control. And there's the whole kidney thing, and the possibility of the transplant rejection will always be in the background. But I love you, Florence, and I want to be with you. I want to make a family with you. I want to help you bring up our baby—and maybe more babies in the future, if we're lucky. I'm hoping that maybe I can stay here permanently, but until a permanent job comes up here I'm happy to commute, or do whatever it takes to make this work. I know you've been hurt, and I know I'm asking you to take a huge risk—but I love you and I think we can make this work if we do this together. Will you marry me?'

He loved her.

He wanted to marry her.

He wanted to be there for the baby, make a family with her.

'You don't have to answer just yet,' he said. 'Think about it. I'll give you all the time you need.'

'You love me,' she said.

'And I'm not asking you to marry me just because of the baby, or because I think it's the right thing to do. I'm asking you because I want *you*. Because with you the world finally makes sense.'

'I've been so scared of letting myself fall for you. That's why I left your hotel room, that morning. I thought you'd be gone again in a few weeks and I didn't want to fall in love with you, only to lose you,' Florence said. 'But I don't think my heart was listening to my head, because I fell in love with you anyway. The way you danced with me. The way you made me feel.' She swallowed hard. 'I love you, Rob. You're right. It's not going to be easy. But we can make this work because we'll be together and we're on the same side. So yes. I'll marry you and make a family with you.'

He whooped, picked her up, and swung her round. And then he put her down hastily. 'Sorry. I need to treat you with kid gloves.'

'Says the man who can't stand cotton wool,' she pointed out.

'I seem to remember someone recommending bamboo cloths,' he said with a grin.

She spread her hands. 'Works for me.'

He kissed her. 'I love you, Florence. I'm going to be the best partner and the best dad I can be—and I know I'll be my best self with you by my side.'

'I love you, too, Rob.'

He kissed her again. 'And I think we have some family meet-ups to arrange. My family's going to love you.'

'And mine's going to love you. Especially

if you tell three certain flower girls that they can have pink floaty dresses.'

'With an accessory of dinosaurs,' he said.

'Yeah. Works for me.' He kissed her again. 'And we have a wedding to plan.'

# EPILOGUE

*August, nine months later*

Florence and Gemma stood still as their matrons of honour did up the zips at the back of their dresses, then came round to the front.

'Beautiful,' Claire pronounced.

'Perfect,' Lexy agreed.

'And we're all ready, girls?' Rupa, Florence's best friend and chief bridesmaid, asked.

'Yes!' Margot, Anna, Scarlett—Gemma's goddaughter—and Darcey chorused, doing a curtsey.

Even baby Iona, cradled in her grandmother's arms, cooed a kind of 'yes'.

'It's a perfect day for a wedding,' Stephanie Baxter, Gemma's mum, said.

'Doubly perfect for a double wedding,' Heidi Jacobs, Florence's mum, added. 'Isn't that right, Iona?'

The baby gurgled again.

Stephanie glanced at her watch. 'Looks as if we're about ready to go. Who's going to hold my hand?'

'Me!' Scarlett said.

'And me!' Anna said.

'I'll let the photographer know we're coming,' Claire said. 'I can't believe you found a house with a double staircase.'

'One side for each bride, and all our bridesmaids and matrons of honour in the middle,' Florence said gleefully. 'Just be glad we didn't make you all dress in Regency outfits.'

'Olls would look lovely as a Regency gentleman,' Gemma said. 'Though Rob would have to lose the stubble and wear a wig.'

'He would've grown over-the-top whiskers, if we'd suggested that,' Florence said with a grin. 'They'll look good enough in top hat and tails.'

'And you look amazing,' Stephanie said. 'Gemma, your father's so thrilled.'

'Me, too,' Gemma said softly.

Florence reached across and squeezed her sister-in-law-to-be's hand; Gemma had told her about how Oliver had helped heal the breach with her parents. 'Hey. No crying allowed, even if they're happy tears.'

'Yeah.' Gemma gave her a broad smile.

'The only one allowed to cry is Iona. And I get first dibs on cuddles.'

Florence saw the sudden brightness in Gemma's eyes, and wondered. When their mums and attendants had all left the room, she said, 'Would I be right in guessing you're just past the morning sickness stage?'

Gemma blushed. 'That's the problem with having medics in the family. They notice things. Twelve weeks.'

'You look doubly radiant—a bride and a mum-to-be,' Florence said. 'Ollie's going to fall in love with you all over again.'

'And Rob's going to fall at your feet. How do you manage to look so gorgeous when you haven't had a full night's sleep in weeks?' Gemma asked.

'Because it's our wedding day,' Florence said, 'so I think there's just a bit of magic everywhere.'

'This place is pretty spectacular,' Rob said, gesturing to the beautiful double staircase in the hall of the Georgian house. There was a stained-glass dome in the ceiling, and the sunlight shone through so that the black and white marble floor was full of colour.

'Given that Gemma loves all the Austen stuff as much as Florence does, we should consider ourselves lucky they were satisfied with a Regency ballroom and didn't want us dressed up as Mr Darcy,' Oliver said with a grin.

'You know what? I wouldn't have minded if it made Florence happy,' Rob said.

'I wouldn't have minded either,' Oliver said. 'Though it's not how or where you get married that matters, it's having your family and your friends there.'

'Agreed,' Rob said. 'Look—here come the girls. I can't believe how many bridesmaids we've got between us. And look at Mum. She looks so happy.'

'Of course she does. It's the wedding day of both of her sons—and she's cuddling her first grandchild,' Oliver said. 'Getting in a bit of pract—' He stopped abruptly. 'Um…'

Rob's head whipped round. 'Are you telling me…?'

'Twelve weeks. Don't tell Gem I told you,' Oliver warned.

'I won't,' Rob promised, and grinned. 'That's brilliant. Welcome to the never-sleep-again club.'

'Thank you. I can't wait,' Oliver said. 'If I look as good on it as you do, bring on the sleepless nights.'

And then they both fell silent as their brides

walked out from opposite sides of the gallery to the middle, hugged each other, then stood at the top of the double staircase.

The string quartet in the middle of the hall began to play 'The Flower Duet' from Delibes' *Lakmé*, and Florence and Gemma walked down the stairs towards them.

'It doesn't get better than this,' Rob whispered.

'Oh, it does,' Oliver said. 'We get to kiss our brides. And the first dance.'

'And then,' Rob said, hugging his brother, 'we get the happy ever after.'

\* \* \* \* \*

*If you missed the previous story in the
Twin Doc's Perfect Match duet,
then check out*

Second Chance with Her Guarded GP

*If you enjoyed this story, check out these
other great reads from Kate Hardy*

Forever Family for the Midwife
Fling with Her Hot-Shot Consultant
Heart Surgeon, Prince...Husband!

*All available now!*